Stilettos and Sins

J.T. Berry

This book is a work of fiction. Any references to historical events, real people, or real places are used fictitiously. Other names, characters, places, and events are products of the author's imagination, and any resemblance to actual events or places or persons, living or dead, is entirely coincidental.

ACKNOWLEDGMENTS

I would like to thank my editor Laura Apger once again for all of her work on and many improvements to this book. The cover was again designed and created by Patrick Knowles, to whom thanks are also due. And special thanks go to LJB yet again for all of her insights and encouragement. Her critical reading made this book much better than it would have been without her. Without her contributions, Dot and Joy would never have come to life.

Chapter One

In ten minutes, it would be 1947, and the party was in full swing. Boisterous, crowded, and glittery, the ballroom was full of excited guests talking and bumping and laughing. In the middle of the room, high above the revolving dancers, a glitter ball at least two feet wide dazzled with blue and green and turquoise sparkles on the faces below. Perfumes and colognes of every confection filled the air.

It was, in short, my worst nightmare.

For the party-goers, Ginnie Townsend's ball was the hot ticket of the season, the place to see and be seen on New Year's Eve. The ballroom of the Beverley Hills Hotel—the Pink Palace to its friends—swirled with the cream of Los Angeles society. Top businessmen, studio moguls, movie stars, and would-be stars rubbed elbows with politicians, socialites with no visible means of support, and probably a couple of mobsters trying to pass as legitimate. A certain famous author, come to Hollywood to slum as a scriptwriter for a private detective movie, was allegedly here. They all mingled around the tables and twirled on the dancefloor. The women were adorned in elegant dresses of every color, some beautifully simple, others as elaborate as wedding cakes, and heels, some so high I was amazed anybody could walk in them, let alone dance. The men wore black-tie, their role merely to provide a backdrop to the ladies' fashion parade.

Voices rose to be heard over the band and the loudness spiraled upwards. Occasional squeals of "Darling!" would portend a near-hug and air kisses between women who did not want to crease their dresses or smudge their perfect make-up. Overly loud laughter and glassy eyes suggested that many guests would barely make it through the next few minutes before struggling back to their beds and collapsing into alcohol-fueled sleep.

I desperately wanted to be anywhere but here. Somewhere quiet with a large glass of rye close at hand, a good book open on my lap, and the gramophone playing Dinah Shore. But Ginnie needed eyes tonight, so there I was, along with my partner Joy D'Amico. Our private investigation business owed everything to her. And more than that, she was a good friend.

At that moment, Ginnie appeared at my shoulder. She looked as stunning as she always did. Her dress was black satin, tight to her body, then flaring out from the knees. The bodice was sequined, with lace sleeves and a matching neckline. It was gorgeous, and she carried it off perfectly. She was made for social occasions, or perhaps vice versa.

"This is for you, Dot," she said, passing me a tumbler holding an inch of pale brown liquid.

"Thanks, but not right now," I said. "I can't drink while I'm working." I continued scanning the crowd.

Ginnie smiled pleasantly, which I assume was for the benefit of anybody watching. "It's iced tea," she replied. "You need to look like you're drinking or people will wonder what's up."

"Clever. Thank you." When this party was over, I was definitely going to need the real thing.

"Anything yet?"

"Nothing. It would be a lot easier if you hadn't invited two hundred of your closest friends here tonight."

Ginnie made eye-contact with one of those friends, and glided over to greet her.

Joy and I were here because somebody in Ginnie's social circle had lately become a pickpocket, perhaps out of financial distress or simply for the thrill of it, and she needed to know who. We figured that tonight's party would be an irresistible opportunity for the thief. I was posing as a guest, wearing a dress borrowed from Ginnie—she insisted that I wear something that was "this season" so that I didn't look out of place—and my favorite black patent leather pumps. I owned several pairs of more elegant stilettos, all gifts from Ginnie, but tonight I needed shoes I could run in if this business ended in a chase.

Joy was around somewhere, dressed as a waitress because, to quote her, dressing like a guest would make her more uncomfortable than a priest in a brothel. Besides, she had pointed out, as a waitress she would be practically invisible and could circulate freely, even eavesdrop on conversations. Nobody pays attention to the staff.

Over by the doors to the ballroom stood the unmistakable figure of our friend Sam Lowry. His regular job was house detective at the Belvedere hotel downtown, but tonight, they would have to make do without him. Over six feet tall, sturdily built, smoking his usual fat cigar, Sam's role tonight was to be noticed. One look at him and your only question would be whether he used to be a cop, or still was. We hoped that if our thief spotted the obvious security detail, he would become complacent about the other eyes—our eyes—on him.

Joy came over to me, carrying a tray of canapés. I picked one up and nibbled on it, just to give my fingers something to do. I stared out across the dance floor, hoping for a break.

"Anything?" she asked.

"Nothing," I replied. "You?"

"Zip."

I glanced up at the clock. It was just a couple of minutes to midnight.

"I'm worried," I said. "When the clock strikes midnight and the balloons drop, it's going to be chaos in here." I set my fake drink down on Joy's tray.

"Perfect cover for somebody to make a few lifts and disappear into the night," she replied.

And then there it was, right in front of my eyes.

I nodded to Joy. "Look at the blonde girl in the dark blue dress with the pleated skirt. She's dancing with the tall, skinny man. Watch."

They turned, bumped into another couple, and almost faster than the eye could follow, she had taken the man's wallet and slipped it between two pleats of her skirt. A hidden pocket, I assumed.

"That was a very smooth lift," said Joy. "I did not expect our dipper to be a girl. Do you think her partner is on it?"

"No," I replied. "Just before that one, she took his wallet too."

"Now what?"

"You get in position. I'll give you a minute, then approach her."

I kept my eyes on the pickpocket while Joy disappeared through the swing doors to the kitchen. There were only two ways out of this ballroom, the main door and through the kitchen. Waiting for Joy in the kitchen were a couple of very tough taxi drivers, former colleagues of hers, just in case things got physical. I opened my purse and pulled out a pair of handcuffs, then squeezed between the dancers and approached the blonde.

"Excuse me miss," I said, "You need to come with me. Let's not make it difficult."

She stared at me wide-eyed, the proverbial deer in the headlights. Her date started to speak. "What the—" But that's as far as he got before the clock struck midnight and the air was suddenly filled with floating confetti, tumbling balloons, and overlapping shouts of "Happy New Year!"
The girl glanced at the ballroom doors, saw Sam's bulky frame, and bolted in the opposite direction. I was surprised by her agility in her spiked heels as she burst balloons with every skip and step. I tried to push past her dance partner to follow her, but he grabbed my shoulder, and shouted, "Hey! Leave her alone!"

I wriggled free, but now, she was several steps ahead of me, all but lost in the crowd. Unlike her stilettos, my supposedly-practical pumps merely squished and squirted the balloons underfoot, throwing my balance this way and that, and I had to pick my path between them. The crowd closed and opened, and I lost sight of her. All I could hope was that she was heading for the kitchen.

At last, I arrived outside the kitchen doors. I steadied myself, plucking confetti from my borrowed dress.

I didn't have to wait long. After barely a minute, the girl reappeared through the door, a grimace on her face. Right behind her was Joy, holding the girl's arm twisted up behind her back.

"They always run, don't they?" said Joy.

We took the remainder of New Year's Day as a holiday, and on the 2nd, we were back in the office. I pulled the file for Ginnie's case from the filing cabinet and added it to the stack of paperwork on my desk. Joy and I had been satisfactorily busy lately, and I had half a dozen final reports to write up and invoices to send out. In theory, Joy should have been doing the same, but paperwork made her brain fizz, she always said. Sometimes I tried to help her out. Her shorthand notes were thoroughly legible, and I didn't mind transcribing them sometimes. She made up for her dislike of paperwork with her willingness to take on legwork. She had also promised to buy the drinks tonight.

My musing was derailed by the bell of the outer door.

"I've got it," said Joy, dropping her *True Crime Stories* magazine into the top drawer of her desk. I wasn't sure how true the stories were, but they were a lot more lurid than most of our cases. For one thing, we hadn't even seen a corpse in over three months. In her magazine stories, a detective could hardly turn around without tripping over one.

She stepped into the waiting room and returned a moment later, followed by a tall, thin, hollow-cheeked man with sparse, receding hair that at first glance, added ten years to his apparent age. He had the characteristic stoop of a man embarrassed to be the tallest in the room. With a second look, I realized he was probably only in his mid-30s. He was wearing a conservatively-cut black suit, white shirt, and narrow black tie, and was crushing the brim of his black fedora in his fingers. In his other hand was a boxy black leather briefcase. He might as well have been wearing a sandwich board announcing himself as a federal bureaucrat.

"Dorothy Stone?" he asked, tentatively.

"That's me," I replied. "But I prefer Dot if we're going to be informal."

"Miss Stone, can I speak with you in private?"

Evidently, we weren't going to be informal.

"If you close the door behind you, that's as private as it gets in here."

He glanced over his shoulder at Joy.

"Sorry, I mean, completely private. Confidential. Classified."

"There's nothing you can say in front of me that you can't say in front of Joy," I told him.

"It's okay," said Joy, picking up on his unspoken discomfort, which I had completely missed. That was normal for me. "I could do with stretching my legs anyway," she continued. She pulled her leather jacket from the coatrack, put on her sunglasses and stepped out, pulling the door shut behind herself. A few seconds later, the bell announced that the outer door had opened and closed.

My visitor was still standing, wringing the brim of his hat. I realized he was waiting for an invitation to sit down. I offered him a seat and poured coffee for both of us. I hoped it would give him something to do with his hands other than ruining his fedora.

"Your colleague," he said. "She was a WASP during the war?"

"B-17s, yes. What tipped you off?"

"The patches on her flight jacket, for one. And the Army Air Forces standard issue Aviators. You can pick up that sort of thing at Army Surplus stores these days, I suppose, but she wore them like she earned them."

"You're observant," I said.

"That's sort of my job," he said, a little more confidence in his voice now. He slid a business card across the desk. There was a printed seal and the words *Department of State* and *Office of Intelligence Research*. Underneath was his name, Mr. Daniel Morgan, and a phone number in Washington, D.C. I rotated the card to face me and carefully centered it on my desk in front of me.

"I thought I knew all the intelligence agencies," I said. I'd been a codebreaker during the war, work that had brought me into contact with just about every branch of intelligence, military or civilian. We didn't just break codes ourselves, we also trained agents in how to use them in the field.

"We used to be part of OSS," he replied.

"Wasn't OSS disbanded at the end of the war?"

"Officially, yes. The field people are now the Central Intelligence Group. And those of us from the Research and Analysis Branch were transferred to State and given our own bureau."

"How is that working out for you?"

"Very nicely, actually. We get to work on a lot of things beyond just military analysis now, and we can have a lot more impact." For the first time, Morgan was starting to look comfortable.

"So what does the bureau want with me?"

"We have a job for you." His voice had become clipped and tense again, all comfort dissipated.

"We should be able to add another case to our workload," I said, "depending on how many hours it needs."

"This would be more of a full-time assignment," he replied.

"I have a full-time job here, Mr. Morgan," I said. He looked around the room, taking in our cramped little office, its two kitty-corner desks, the well-used coffee machine, the overflowing ashtrays, and the row of filing cabinets, admittedly mostly still filled with air. I had no idea what he made of it all, but I was proud of what Joy and I had established. It had taken several months to get here, and a lot of financial support from Ginnie, but *D'Amico and Stone, Private Investigations* was finally paying its own way. I had no interest in disrupting that.

He looked like I'd kicked his cat, not turned down his job offer. "Miss Stone, it would not be hyperbolic of me to say that this is a matter of national security." From the tension wringing his face like a cheap dishcloth, it was clear he didn't like having to be assertive. I worried for his hat again.

"I expect everything your bureau does is literally a matter of national security," I replied. "But the war's over and I did my part. I have a life of my own now. A partner. Friends. And a business. I'm not going to set all that aside and run off to Washington."

It was an uncharitable thought, but I couldn't help feeling that the bureau had sent the wrong man for this job. I felt sorry for him, but that wasn't a good reason to change my mind.

He sighed. "I don't suppose you know of somebody else I might approach?"

"It would help if I knew what the assignment was," I pointed out.

"It's very sensitive, so there's a limit to what I can tell you. What do you know about Operation Paperclip?"

"Only what I read in the papers. Nazi scientists recruited to work on American research projects." *Those people should be in prison, not government jobs*, I thought to myself.

"Yes, well, we prefer you say 'German' rather than 'Nazi'. In theory, war criminals and high-ranking party officials were disqualified, although it seems some people's sins are more forgivable than others. In any case, the government is deeply concerned about losing ground militarily to the Soviets. They have their own Germans. But we think ours are better."

"Why do you say that?"

"Because most German scientists were terrified of finding themselves working for the Soviet Union, under prison conditions and the constant threat of deportation to a gulag in Siberia. Any that could get away made their way westward to surrender to the advancing Americans or British in the hope of better treatment. So we had our pick of the best minds." He paused. "It's not so widely known, but we even whisked away some top targets from the Soviet sector before the Russians could round them up. Quite a coup, really."

"And what's the assignment?"

"I can't say much about that. Only that it requires somebody with analytical skills like yours, excellent German, and who can pass a stringent security check. You already did, by the way. Most of all, it has to be somebody outside the current intelligence community. If I told you more, you'd understand why I can't tell you more."

It was annoyingly incomplete, the kind of mystery that made my brain itch in places I couldn't scratch, a familiar sensation from when I had worked in intelligence. Information was obsessively compartmentalized, and for good reason. I knew better than to press for more detail.

I gave his request some thought. He waited patiently for me.

"Barbara Watson," I finally said. "Sharp as a razor, and the best cryptanalyst I ever worked alongside. If you think you want me, she's better. She used to live in Hoboken, New Jersey. I don't know where she is now."

Morgan jotted a quick note. "Don't worry, I'm sure we'll be able to locate her."

I didn't doubt it. I stood up and shook his hand. He gathered up his hat and briefcase.

"I'll see myself out," he said.

I waited to hear the bell of the outer door. I added his card to the collection in my top drawer, then took a case folder off the pile in my inbox. I didn't open it. I was feeling the tiniest pang of nostalgia for my days as a codebreaker. The work had been challenging, as well as extremely important for the war effort. More than that, it had been the first place I had really felt I belonged, surrounded by smart women whose minds worked like mine. I had been forced to quit when my father had died, leaving me to take over his bookstore, and I belatedly realized I should have made more effort to stay in touch with my former colleagues.

The outer bell rang again, and Joy announced her return. The moment passed. I had another life now, and I certainly couldn't see myself spending the rest of my career as a cryptanalyst, with no hope of advancement in the post-war army.

Most of all, if I had stayed in Intelligence, I would never have had my friendship with Joy.

Joy came in and hung up her flight jacket. "I guess you can't tell me what that was about?" she asked.

"I barely know myself," I sighed.

"Do you want to knock off early and go to Jack's for a drink?"

Jack's was our bar, a genuine spit-and-sawdust, working man's kind of joint. The sign in the window said "we never close" and I had not yet had reason to doubt it. Joy had taken me there when we first met and introduced me to her cabbie co-workers. Now I was considered a regular there, a position I never could have imagined before I met Joy.

"Absolutely," I said, and put the case folder back on the pile.

CHAPTER TWO

I thought I'd seen the last of Mr. Morgan. I was wrong. A month later, he was back in my office, sitting across my desk. The dark circles around his eyes suggested he had not been sleeping well.

"Barbara turned you down, I take it," I said.

He took a deep breath. "I'm sorry to tell you this, but Miss Watson is dead."

I took a moment for myself before responding. Barbara had been a good colleague and as much of a friend to me as anybody on the team.

"So now you're back to me. But my position hasn't changed, I'm afraid."

"I have a proposition that perhaps you'll find more acceptable. Come and work on the project for two weeks. That way, I can read you in fully. I'm confident once you understand how critical the work is, you'll agree to see it through."

I leaned back in my chair. Two weeks was a more manageable commitment. Curiosity about the project wrestled with reluctance to invest so much in a single job, without even knowing what it was.

"I'll have to make sure Joy is okay with me leaving her to run the whole business, even for just two weeks. But I'm willing to consider it."

"Will you call me when you have a decision?"

"Of course. Probably as soon as tomorrow. I don't let big decisions linger."

He wrote down a local phone number for me.

After Morgan had left, I sat and examined my own feelings. I was still absorbing the news about Barbara, but I set that aside for later. I needed to focus on Morgan's proposal. Two weeks would be alright, and two weeks of full-time work would certainly get our year off to a good start financially. The agency—and the rest of my life—would still be here when I returned. Regardless of how I felt about Operation Paperclip, it was going to carry on regardless of what I thought or what the *New York Times* wrote. Perhaps the job was even something worthwhile. For instance, it would be satisfying to root out anybody who had faked their way through the denazification reeducation that they were supposedly required to take. Perhaps I was talking myself into saying yes.

My brain nagged away at the question for the rest of the day. When five o'clock came around, Joy and I walked over to Jack's. Seated on a couple of stools with beer and rye in front of us and cigarettes lit—Kool for me and Lucky Strike for her, as usual—was where we often did our best thinking.

"This is difficult," I told her, "because I'm going to ask you whether you're okay with something I can't tell you anything about."

"I get it," Joy replied. "Government stuff."

"I'd be gone for two weeks, and even I don't know what I'd be doing. You'll have to run the whole place by yourself, and handle whatever business walks in."

"Can I save all the paperwork for when you get back?"

As so often happened with Joy, I wasn't sure if she was serious, joking, or somewhere in between.

"I suppose I'd owe you that," I replied.

We clinked our glasses to seal the deal. And just like that, I had committed myself to Morgan's cloak and dagger mission. Although I hoped there wouldn't be any daggers. As I nursed my second rye, I mulled over how odd it felt for me to be asking for Joy's blessing. I'd been so self-reliant for most of my life, it was unusual for me to have to even consider somebody else's needs. On the other hand, I wouldn't be doing this at all—along with a lot of other things—if it wasn't for Joy. Our friendship was changing me—or perhaps, it was bringing out parts of me I had long repressed. I just hoped I wouldn't lose my self-sufficiency along the way.

I called Morgan first thing the next morning. He asked me to come over to his office. I rode the Red Line over to the Civic Center and was there in 30 minutes. The Federal Building he was working out of was just one block away from police headquarters, where my boyfriend Eddie was stationed. Eddie Ramirez was a homicide detective; we'd met during the Helen James case last summer and had been dating ever since. I thought about calling in after I was done with Morgan, just in case he was in the office and free to take a coffee break. The chances were slim, but if I was going to be gone for two weeks, I really wanted to talk with him before I left. Better to see him for dinner, I decided.

Morgan was wearing the same suit and tie as before, and what I assumed was a different white shirt. I guessed he didn't put a lot of thought into what to wear to the office each day, an approach I thoroughly empathized with.

"I'm surprised you have an office out here," I told him. "I expected you'd all be in D.C. and the raw intelligence would come to you."

"It's temporary," he explained. "This is a former OSS office. It was useful at the time to be close to the defense contractors here, the west coast naval bases, and the training camp on San Catalina. But OSS was disbanded with literally ten days notice, so we haven't all relocated yet. For now, we're still sharing the space with our CIG colleagues."

He led me into a small conference room with the usual worse-for-wear government issue table and a half a dozen threadbare chairs. Another man was sitting there, at the head of the conference table. He was physically unremarkable, a man of average height and thinning hair, paunchy, aged perhaps forty. Although his suit looked fairly new, it squeezed him around the middle, his belt straining to keep his gut in. *A middle-aged man rapidly going to seed,* I thought.

He stood to greet me, holding out his chubby, sausage-fingered hand. "Miss Stone, I'm Director Wardour," he said. His mouth smiled but his eyes did not.

"Mr. Wardour is my boss," explained Morgan. "He's the one that brought us in on this mission."

"I just wanted to stop in and thank you for taking this project on," said Wardour. "It's very patriotic of you."

I wasn't sure what I was supposed to reply to that. "You're welcome" seemed inappropriate, especially since I still didn't know what I was signing up to, but the extended silence certainly suggested I was expected to say something.

Wardour and Morgan both started to fidget, which I took to mean that the silence was now uncomfortably long for them.

I realized I needed to put them out of their discomfort. "Of course," I said. It seemed suitably vague and noncommittal.

With that, Wardour excused himself and left the room. A woman came in carrying a stack of forms. She was very pretty—tall, slim, and very blonde with piercing blue eyes—and in any town other than Hollywood, would probably be considered beautiful.

I held out my hands to take the paperwork from her. She glared icily at me, and dumped the pile on the table with a hefty thud. I dug my pen out of my purse and started on the forms. Most of them were familiar from when I'd signed up during the war. The woman stood close behind me, looking over my shoulder while I completed the task, making the hairs on the back of my neck prickle. As soon as I had finished, she picked up the stack, turned on her heel, and stalked out without saying a word.

"What was that about?" I asked Morgan, perplexed.

He sighed. "That was Mary McCardy. She's our secretary. Well, strictly speaking, she's Wardour's secretary, but she does admin for the whole team."

"She doesn't seem very happy about it," I remarked.

"Just between us, I suspect she wanted this assignment for herself. But Wardour insisted we use an outsider."

"So now can you tell me what this is all about?" I asked.

"As I mentioned before, it involves Operation Paperclip," he began. "The army has assigned a number of the German scientists and engineers to an Army Air Forces research facility at Wright Field, near Dayton, Ohio."

"What are they working on?"

"Jet aircraft. Reverse engineering captured German planes, and developing new ones for us. Please don't ask me about the technical details. The problem is, somebody is passing classified information from the program to the Soviets."

"How do you know?"

He paused. I assumed he was carefully formulating an answer that told me no more than I absolutely needed to know.

"As I said before, the Soviets have their own version of Paperclip. And we know that some of our documents and designs are in their hands."

"You have spies inside their labs?" I asked.

"Our enemies have spies. We have assets," he replied, smiling. It was the first time I'd seen him do so. Perhaps that was a running joke among his bureau colleagues. "Anyway, my bureau was asked to analyze the leaks to see if we could identify the source."

"What did you learn?"

"That our spy is being very careful about what he chooses to leak. The leaked documents point to a variety of different researchers and no obvious research agenda. So much so, in fact, it feels deliberate. We think he's been warned about the trail he might leave."

"Warned by whom? His handler?"

"Well, that brings us around to why you're here. We believe he has a collaborator, likely an American on the base. Probably in the military, possibly even in Intelligence. Somebody who knows our methods and will see us coming."

"Ah," I said. I couldn't think of anything better.

"So we need somebody inside the program who can observe without raising suspicion, and identify the spy. And ideally, his collaborator too. It can't be done by anybody from the intelligence services, because we have no idea who might be compromised. The fact that you're an experienced investigator is a huge bonus, which is why I came to you first."

I reflected on the irony of that last qualification. I'd been an investigator for barely a year, and a professional for only half of that. I did not feel like I had earned the compliment 'experienced.'

"What about the FBI? Aren't they supposed to investigate this kind of thing?"

"In theory, yes. The problem is Hoover. He's a glory hound, and whenever his boys catch a spy, he makes sure the story is all over the newspapers with his name in the headlines and his picture underneath. There's enough public hostility to Paperclip already. We don't need that kind of publicity."

"I suppose that makes sense."

He handed me two thin files.

"This one is your cover," he said. "It's basically your own life, to make it easy to remember, minus the fact that you've become a private investigator. In this version, you closed the bookstore and rejoined the military because the shop wasn't making money."

That certainly ran close to the truth. The bookstore had been on its last legs financially before Ginnie had bailed me out and Joy and I had opened the agency.

"Your previous military service was as a simple administrator, not a cryptographer. And don't let on that you speak German. If they don't know, they might get careless around you."

I flicked open the file.

"I'm going to be a filing clerk?" I said, not hiding my distaste.

"Yes, I'm sorry. I know it's well beneath your capabilities, but you need to blend in, not stand out, and admin is what the majority of women in the military are doing now the war is over."

I tried to set aside my irritation by reminding myself I was only playing a part. Joy and I had both done it before.

"On the plus side, you'll be a civilian contractor, so you won't have to wear a uniform," he added.

"And I'm using my own name?"

"Yes, it makes the story practically bulletproof if somebody checks up on it. Short of somebody walking down your street and knocking on the door of your detective agency, this will stand up to scrutiny. And it's a lot easier for you to stay in character than if we asked you to play a role. Elaborate legends are best reserved for experienced field agents."

I nodded. I deferred to his expertise on that.

"The other file is background on the key people you'll meet at the facility, both Germans and Americans," he continued, "plus some other information about the facility you'll be expected to know. You can read these here, but they can't leave this room," he said. "You'll just have to remember the key information as best you can."

I didn't bother to tell him that my best meant that I'd remember practically every single word and punctuation mark, including the typos, of which I had noticed two already.

"Captain Hathaway is my contact on the base?" I asked.

"Yes. He knows who you are and why you're there. He's Military Intelligence, not one of us, so he's on a strictly need-to-know basis."

"And what does he need to know?"

"Nothing."

"Okay. What do I do if I uncover something? Or need guidance?"

"We have a contact protocol. Find a phone somewhere private and call this number. It's monitored day and night," he said, sliding a note across the table to me.

I committed it to memory.

"Nobody will answer, but let it ring," he continued. "When it disconnects, it means we traced your number."

"Why would you need to trace my number?" I asked.

"We'll call you back through a secure switchboard, so we don't need to worry about a civilian operator listening in."

"What hours can I reach you?"

"Eight in the morning till eight at night, your time. Outside of those hours, somebody else will call you back."

"What if you need to contact me?"

"We'll get a message to you somehow, but we won't do so unless absolutely necessary, because of the risk of exposing you. It's better if you check in every couple of days, even if you have nothing to report."

It all sounded a bit convoluted, but I had to trust the process. "You're making this sound rather more dangerous than I initially supposed."

"This is just standard protocol for the protection of any asset in the field. One last thing, though. Don't trust anybody there, however harmless they seem. Not even the project's own security people. Anybody could be compromised. Your safety depends on everybody believing you are simply an administrative assistant."

"My safety? Okay, now I'm worried again."

He smiled again, but it was a thin, grim smile.

That night, I met Eddie for dinner at a place in Chinatown that was a favorite of ours. Every time we went there, the owner told Eddie it was on the house, but he insisted on paying. Eddie had told me that a lot of cops leaned on restaurants and bars for free food and drink. They treated it as a perk of the job. But in his mind, it was no better than protection money. To him, there was no such thing as minor corruption; once you started down that road, small acts became larger ones and before you knew it, you were shooting suspects and planting guns on them as justification, or looking the other way when corrupt politicians and powerful interests asked you to. As far as Eddie was concerned, he either did the job right or not at all.

It was one of the reasons I loved him. And sometime soon I was going to have to tell him that out loud, but I was still hoping he would say it first. I'd never said it to a man before, and I really didn't want the first time to go badly.

As we ate—Eddie confidently with chopsticks, me with a fork, because I was anxious about dropping food in my lap—I told him what little I could, and that I would not be able to call him while I was undercover.

"I get it," he said. "Every contact with your real life is a risk. I've run C.I.s, and it's not that different." I must have looked blank, because he continued, "Confidential informants. Criminals who inform on their colleagues to us, in return for some past crimes being overlooked. And in some cases, ongoing crimes."

Eddie did not look happy about that last part but, he explained, sometimes you had to let the small fish go to catch the bigger ones.

"How are you feeling about this whole thing?" he asked. "I'm guessing this is very new for you."

I put my fork down and stared at my lap. "Actually, I'm having a few jitters already. I might have bitten off more than I can chew."

"You'll be fine once you're on the ground," said Eddie. He rested a reassuring hand on my forearm. He was one of the few people who could touch me without startling me. Somehow, his hands always felt supporting, never restraining. "You're smart, strong, and resilient. Observe everything, and analyze relentlessly, just like you always do. And whatever it is you're up to, the basics never change: means, motive, opportunity."

I was always amazed at the trust Eddie had in my abilities, and grateful for how he helped me trust myself. I got up from my seat, stepped around the table, and kissed him firmly on the lips. It was a show of affection I almost never made in public, but the moment—and Eddie—deserved it..

"You're the best," I told him. And I resolved to tell him the other thing when I got back from this assignment.

Chapter Three

The following Sunday found me stepping off a bus five miles outside Dayton, Ohio, clutching an oversized cheap cardboard suitcase. My trench coat was wrapped tight against the cold. It was early evening, the temperature barely above freezing, and my LA wardrobe was completely inadequate for an Ohio winter. I was standing outside the gates of Wright Field, home to the Army Air Forces' Technical Data Laboratory; a collection of captured advanced German aircraft; and most importantly for my purposes, a group of over one hundred German scientists and engineers, with more arriving every week. I was under strict instructions from Morgan to keep my personal opinions about the project—and the Germans—to myself. Apparently, it was a very touchy subject.

I took in what I could of the camp in the thin dusk light. To both sides of the entranceway, a chain link fence, about twelve feet high and supported by metal posts every twenty feet or so, disappeared into the deepening twilight. The fence was topped by vicious razor wire. Behind it was a grassy gap of ten feet before a second fence. The entrance itself consisted of two small prefab huts, one on each side of a roadway that was blocked by a pair of lifting arm barriers painted red and white. I guessed that leaving the base was controlled as rigorously as entering it. Beyond the second fence, drab, boxy buildings, made from cement or cinder block by the look of them, receded into the dark.

The guards in the booth waved me forward and I presented the paperwork that claimed I was to be a technical administrative aide for the project. Taking pity on my shivers, they invited me to come inside the booth while they checked my name against their list of expected arrivals. Apparently, they had decided I wasn't much of a security threat. One of them handed me a lanyard with a pass attached. The other picked up a phone, spoke briefly, then told me to wait.

My curiosity got the better of me. "What's the gap between the fences for?" I asked.

"Landmines, miss," replied one of the men. His face was completely deadpan. I wasn't sure if he was making fun of me, and decided to keep my other questions to myself.

About ten minutes later, a military staff car pulled up, skidding to a stop on the wet pavement. For the first time in many years, I was at a loss to identify a car. Makes and models had been a fascination of mine since childhood, and I thought I knew everything on the road. But this car was sort of custom vehicle for the military, it seemed, painted drab olive with a white Army star stenciled on the side. The woman behind the wheel lowered her window and waved me over. I scurried over to the car, threw my suitcase in the back, slipped into the passenger seat, and slammed the door shut behind me. Thankfully, the heater was on full blast.

"Hi, I'm Caroline! Welcome to the TDL!" bubbled the woman. She was about my height, slim, and extremely cheerful.

I immediately hoped we would not be rooming together. She executed a rapid K turn and pulled away, spinning the wheels on the wet tarmac. I feared that her confidence behind the wheel exceeded her ability.

"You're Dot, right? That's great!" she continued excitedly. "We're going to be roomies. I already bagged the top bunk. Sorry about that!"

"I'm sure I'll manage," I replied. I hoped that didn't come across as sarcastic. Tone was difficult for me, even when I liked people, and I already doubted that I was going to like Caroline.

"Mess hall already started, so we'll head right over and drop your bag later. You'll meet some of the girls tonight, and the rest over the next few days. I just know you're going to love it here. All of the girls are really nice."

"What about the researchers?"

"Oh, the usual mix. Most of them are fine, but there are some that are very snobbish to anybody who isn't a rocket scientist."

"I thought they were working on jet planes here?" I replied, wrinkling my forehead in confusion.

Caroline giggled, a little tinkling laugh that I was going to have to try very hard not to kill her over. "It's just an expression they have here. It means somebody who is very smart."

"Oh, okay. I guess there's a lot of jargon I'm going to have to pick up."

"That reminds me, one more thing. The Germans are very fussy about who's a scientist and who's an engineer and who's a technician. It's like a whole class system for them. So if you see somebody with 'Doctor' on their badge, you absolutely must call them 'Herr Doctor.' Oh, and don't ask any of them what they did in the war, obviously."

"Because when the answer is 'murdered Jews and bombed children', it makes the whole conversation awkward?" I asked.

This time she laughed throatily. "Oh my goodness, you're a cut-up!" she said. "Just don't say things like that in front of anybody but me, okay? The Germans have absolutely no sense of humor, and some of the other girls are tattles."

Her energy was exhausting. If we were going to be bunking together, I might have to pretend to be asleep every time she came into the room.

She pulled the car up in front of a low hut with steamed-up windows and we scurried inside before the cold could bite too hard, a freezing draft tight on our tails. I was immediately overwhelmed by the noise, heat, and humidity. I followed Caroline over to a counter that was doling out military grade hash, and then to a table where half a dozen women were already forking through watery mashed potatoes and some concoction of ground beef in gravy.

"Caroline!" called out one of them. "We saved you two places."

"Thanks, Maggie!" replied Caroline.

Caroline introduced me and then the others went around the table saying their names, which I knew I would not remember. I had a preternatural memory for many things, but names routinely eluded me. The only one that stuck was Ali, a thin, pale woman, her black hair cut in a simple bob that framed her high cheekbones. She stood out as the only one not to have her hair in an elaborate arrangement that reminded me of the wartime fashion for curls and waves.

Caroline saw my discomfort and came to my rescue. "Don't worry," she said, "nobody expects you to remember all that the first time. And when we are working, everybody is 'Miss So-and-so' around the Germans, so you can check their badges if you forget."

The conversation immediately reverted to what I assumed was base gossip. Names and events were tossed around that meant nothing to me, and conversations crossed each other and made it impossible to follow any one of them. I noticed Ali wasn't joining in, and barely seemed to be paying attention. I wondered what was on her mind. And then I considered that perhaps, like me, she tended to be withdrawn in noisy, busy groups. It would be nice to find somebody like-minded here.

I took the opportunity to check out the rest of the room. Most of the other tables were filled with a mixture of more girls intermingled with men in suits and in some cases white lab coats. There were a couple of handfuls of men in officers' uniforms scattered around too. I supposed that the enlisted men ate elsewhere.

I nudged Caroline. "Who are those four?" I asked, nodding towards a group of stiff-backed men with short cropped hair sitting at a large table by themselves.

"Those are the hardline enn-ay-zee-ayes," said Caroline. "We have to work with them, but nobody wants to socialize with them, not even the other Germans."

"I thought that… those people… were excluded from the program?" I had heard Morgan's view on that, but I wanted to hear how the people here felt too.

"It turns out the rules are flexible for people who are really valuable. None of us are happy about it."

"But why are they working for the Americans?"

"Because the alternative is to be sent back to Germany to face trial, or repatriated to the Soviet Sector. They're a real pain, by the way. They keep bugging me for dates and I keep saying no. Apparently, they decided I fit their Aryan ideal of womanhood."

She looked me over. "You're probably going to get the same, I'm afraid. Whatever you do, don't go blonde."

"I'm going to be a huge disappointment to them, then," I replied. "I'm not planning to be somebody's *Hausfrau* who stays home, has babies, and cooks strudel, least of all for an unrepentant Na-… you know." I silently cursed myself for letting slip a word of German, and hoped nobody would make anything of it. It was a tiny slip, but as they'd drilled into us during the war, the smallest mistakes can cost lives.

"And what about that man sitting all alone?" I continued quickly.

"That's Eckert. He's the big cheese around here. You don't sit with him unless he invites you to."

"Good to know," I said, and returned to trying to force down my Government Issue slop. After a long day of travel, I was just about hungry enough.

After dinner, we returned to the car for my bag. Caroline had parked it as close as she could to our dormitory, so we walked the remaining short distance.

"The other women here, did they volunteer or were they assigned by the Army?" I asked as we walked, me lugging my suitcase, her with her arms folded across her chest. Both our heads were lowered against the wind.

"Most of them were assigned from other departments after a security check. A few of us asked for the assignment. Ali, me, a couple of others. You, I guess?"

"Why did you ask for this gig?"

"I wanted to feel like I was doing something worthwhile, not just filing and typing in some administrative office. And this feels like as close as I can get to something important."

"I understand that," I said. "There aren't a lot of opportunities for us now that the war is over. The government definitely wants to put us back in our boxes."

I reflected ruefully that for a few years, women had been doing everything from driving trucks to building battleships. And our reward for all that hard work was to be told to put our aprons back on and bake a cake. It was especially galling after we had proved ourselves capable of so much, often in jobs that the men had assumed we would not be able to do. But now the message—from the government and from Madison Avenue alike—was that the way for a woman to be most valuable to society was to raise her husband's children to be good Americans. American men had won the war, but American women had lost the peace.

"Anyway," continued Caroline, "You can sit where you like tomorrow, but I hope you'll sit with us again."

I was conflicted. On the one hand, I didn't want Caroline to think I was snubbing her. But mealtimes were also an opportunity to gather intelligence from whoever I was sitting with, which meant I'd benefit from spreading myself around as much as possible. I would have to figure that out in the morning. It was the kind of social nuance I was not equipped to navigate in the moment.

We had reached the dormitory now. Inside, Caroline led me down a hallway to the room we would share.

"Bathroom's at the end of the corridor," she told me. "It's all a bit communal and there's not a lot of privacy, but you'll get used to it."

Sharing showers was not exactly comfortable for me, but I had managed to work through it in college. I could manage it again.

Caroline unlocked the door to our room. "People are quite social around here, so if you're ever in the middle of something and don't want anybody to interrupt, tie a scarf on the door." She gave me a theatrical wink, and after a couple of seconds, I realized what she was implying.

Our room was small, basic, but perfectly adequate. As promised, there were bunk beds, plus a writing desk, a bookcase (empty apart from a well-thumbed copy of Gone With the Wind—Caroline was evidently not much of a reader), and a cupboard. All of it had a simple design that hinted at wartime construction. The floor of the room was wooden with a faded woolen rug covering most of it.

Caroline opened the cupboard doors. "You get the left half," she said. She had cleared about one quarter of the rail.

It only took me a couple of minutes to stash my few clothes and stack my suitcase with Caroline's on top of the cupboard. My wardrobe mostly consisted of a handful of plain, durable dresses appropriate to an underpaid working girl, and one nice dress for social occasions. Caroline looked over my staid selection and did not hide her disdain.

"Those are all very stodgy, aren't they?" she said. "If you want to borrow something of mine with a bit more flair, just ask. We're about the same size."

I kept my face as neutral as I could. It was far too early to be making enemies and stocking up grudges.

"Oh," she added, "I should show you this too." She indicated a couple of bulky hooded coats in military green hanging on the back of the door. "Take whichever one you want. You're going to need a good anorak around here," she said. "That raincoat isn't going to do much in these temperatures."

I reflected that it wasn't the most elegant coat I'd ever seen, but from my brief experience of Dayton's winter weather, it was more than welcome. With its fur lining and three-quarter length, it was technically a parka, not an anorak, but I suspected that Caroline would not be interested in the distinction. Nor possibly anybody else within several miles of us.

"So what do people here do after dinner?" I asked.

"There's not a whole lot, I'm afraid. There's a social club for the officers and scientists, and another one for the enlisted men. We're allowed in either, depending on what kind of company you want. I try to not go every single night, because it's almost impossible not to drink there. There's always a man wanting to buy you one. Each of the dorms has its own common room, and you'll usually find a few people hanging around there. There's a movie theater, but it's just the one movie for two weeks at a time. And if you want to be by yourself, you can stay here and listen to the radio."

"What about going into town?"

"It's possible, but the last bus back here is before ten during the week. So we usually only go in on the weekends, unless we can get a date with a car to drive us. You'll have to be nice to the officers; they can requisition cars sometimes."

"But you had a car to pick me up," I said.

"I smiled sweetly at a sergeant from the motor pool, and promised not to take it off the base."

"Shouldn't you return it?"

"Oh, I'm sure they'll find it in the morning," she said carelessly.

I'd had enough of people for one day, I decided. The bureau had bought me a plane ticket to Dayton Municipal airport, but even so, I'd been traveling all weekend, spending the night in Dallas. After that, the bus ride out here had been over an hour of stop-start. It was better than spending three days or more on Greyhounds, but still it had been exhausting. I plopped myself onto the lower bunk and picked up one of the books I'd brought with me.

"If it's okay with you, I'm going to stay in and read tonight. I can start meeting everybody tomorrow."

"Suit yourself," she said. "I'll try not to wake you when I get back."

Left to myself, I changed into my nightgown and tried to focus on The Grapes of Wrath, but after re-reading the same paragraph three times and still not knowing what it said, I gave up. I lay back and worried about how I was going to pursue this investigation. None of my usual tools were available to me. There were no open records I could search, I couldn't interview people formally, and I could hardly follow people around to see what they were up to. I started to wonder if I was in over my head. On reflection, this assignment was probably better suited to Joy's skills than mine. She had a knack for getting people to open up, and that was a complete mystery to me. But it was a little late to be thinking about that now.

Maybe I should go back to fundamentals, like Eddie had said: means, motive, and opportunity. What could motivate somebody to betray their country? Money and blackmail were two obvious reasons. But in this case, I had to remember that for a lot of people on base, this wasn't even their country. Morgan had suggested that there might be a Russian agent in place. That could mean an actual undercover agent from Russia, rather than an American who had been "turned." And who knew where the Germans' loyalties lay?

My thoughts were still chasing each other when I finally fell asleep. I didn't hear Caroline come in.

Chapter Four

On Monday morning, Caroline took me over to the administrative block and left me in the care of Mrs. Worthington, the supervisor there. She was a stout, matronly woman in her late forties with a rigid expression and an unsympathetic air. I would soon learn that under that harsh exterior was an interior equally harsh. She was dressed stiffly, as if she were trying to imitate an army uniform, and her demeanor matched. If she was trying for 'efficient competence' she was nailing it.

"According to your file, you're qualified in typing and shorthand," she said curtly, "and you have a good head for numbers and organization. You will help Miss Babinski with filing personnel records and research reports. You'll also be responsible for timesheets and attendance logs for the men, as well as the other girls. Your predecessor had a system, supposedly, but I have no idea what it was, so you'll just have to work it out for yourself."

"Yes, ma'am," I said. I wrestled down a strange urge to curtsey.

She handed me a set of keys for the filing cabinets. "Keep these with you at all times. Under no circumstances should anybody else ever touch them," she told me sternly.

"Thank you, Mrs. Worthington," I said. Free access to the personnel records was a big break, although I assumed that the really juicy stuff about what people had done in Germany would not be here, but off in an OSS office somewhere. Or at the Central Intelligence Group, as I would have to get used to calling them now. I wondered whether

Morgan had pulled some strings to get me this specific assignment.

"Miss Babinksi will answer any questions you have, once she drags herself in."

I glanced up at the clock. It was still fifteen minutes before nine.

"If you need anything she can't deal with, come and see me," Mrs. Worthington continued. "My office door is always closed, so knock and wait before coming in."

I took that to mean not to bother her unless the building was burning down and I needed her orders on which files to risk my life for. Mrs. Worthington disappeared into her office, closing the frosted glass door emphatically behind her.

I took stock of where I would be spending my days for the next couple of weeks. There were two desks in the room, arranged back to back. Each had a typewriter with a dust cover, an in-tray, and an out-tray. One of them also had a coffee mug and a small collection of pencils and erasers. I assumed that was Babinski's. I opened a drawer on the other one and dropped my purse inside. Around the room were banks of filing cabinets, military issue gray, and off in a corner by itself was a melamine-topped table with a coffee machine. I decided that I would get some coffee started while I waited for my colleague to arrive and explain what exactly I was supposed to be doing here.

Babinski, it turned out, was Ali, which was a relief. I had identified her as a potential kindred soul over dinner the previous night, and I hoped I would be proven right. She seemed to be the only one not swept up in silly gossip. It made me wonder why she was even friends with Caroline.

"Ali, right?" I said, then immediately glanced over my shoulder in case Mrs. Worthington was about to emerge and chide me for being too informal. "I'm Dot."

"I remember," she said. She peered at my badge. "Stone. Good solid name."

I wasn't sure if she was making a joke or just nervous small talk.

"Babinski is a Polish name, isn't it?" I asked. I wasn't good at small talk, but this seemed like a safe response.

"Yes, it is. And Ali is short for Alicja, which nobody here can pronounce right, so do not even try. You are Barbara's replacement, I think?"

I paused. Could she possibly mean Barbara Watson, my friend whom I had recommended to Morgan? Had she come here before Morgan had returned to recruit me? Morgan had, I reflected, avoided saying anything about how or when Barbara had died. Surely it couldn't have been here; wouldn't he would have told me before sending me into the same situation that had killed Barbara? I had to tread carefully here, and not admit to knowing more than I should.

"I suppose so. What happened to Barbara?" I asked.

"She was killed in a traffic accident in town," said Ali.

Again, I tried to hide what I was feeling behind a professional mask, just as I had so often done when dealing with bookstore customers.

Ali lowered her voice to a conspiratorial whisper. "Some people think that story is a cover-up. Caroline's theory is that Barbara eloped with a Russian."

"Why a Russian?"

"Caroline thinks maybe she was a spy. There are always rumors here that there is a spy among us trying to steal our secrets. But I think it is just something they say to keep us strict about security."

"And what do you think?"

"That probably the official story is true. Why would they lie about something like that? Or maybe Barbara just could not stand working with war criminals and left, and they hushed it up so the rest of us do not get the same idea."

I wasn't sure if the last part was intended as dark humor.

"Are the Germans really that bad?"

"As long as you mind your manners and do what they need, they are mostly respectful. Some of them get bad tempered if you are too slow with your shorthand or make too many mistakes in typing up their reports. It is very unfair. I do not know how we are supposed to know the technical jargon they use. Honestly, I think they are making a lot of it up as they go," she pouted.

I felt like I should drop the subject there in case I seemed too curious. Ali had me unlock one of the filing cabinets.

"This is where the unfiled records go overnight. Everything is locked away whenever we are not here, for confidentiality. Once they are processed, they go into these other cabinets. I will show you what we do with the timesheets, the requisitions, and the personnel reports. The ones on the other wall are for research reports and notes. For now, I will take care of those."

"What about that cabinet?" I said, pointing at a tall, black metal cabinet on the other wall, next to the door to Mrs. Worthington's office.

"Those files are outside our classification. Only Mrs. Worthington has a key for those."

I nodded. My curiosity was piqued.

I spent the rest of the day working my way through the filing backlog that had built up and trying to push intrusive thoughts about Barbara away. *You don't even know if it's your Barbara*, I repeatedly told myself. *It's a very common name.*

A few minutes before five, Ali helped me put everything away securely and lock up the file cabinets. The protocol was strict: I went along the row, locking each in turn, and Ali followed behind double-checking. Mrs. Worthington would lock the office door when she left, Ali explained. I immediately put Mrs. Worthington at the top of my mental list of people who had the opportunity to access the research reports. She had all the keys, she was last to leave, and who knew what she had squirreled away in that enigmatic black cabinet?

"Should we say goodnight to Mrs. Worthington?" I asked. A light was on behind the frosted glass.

"Absolutely not," said Ali. "She does not do social things with low staff like us."

"Good to know," I replied, and mentally filed that too. "Hey, is there somewhere I can make a phone call? I should really let my family know I arrived okay."

"Of course. There are payphones in the officers' club. You can make your call, and then afterwards, we can take a drink before dinner."

It was a ten minute walk over to the club. I was beginning to get a sense of how big the base was.

"The phones are over there," said Ali, pointing to the back corner on the opposite wall from the bar.

I was happy to see there were booths, so I would have some privacy.

"What will you drink?" she asked. "I will get it while you call."

"Rye, please," I told her.

I slipped into one of the phone booths, closed the concertina door, and asked the operator to connect me to Morgan's number. As he'd instructed, I let it ring until it disconnected, then hung up. I hoped he was working late. I needn't have fretted. His callback came thirty seconds later.

I picked up.

"Morgan," said the voice on the other end.

"Stone," I replied.

"I'm surprised to be hearing from you so soon. What's up?"

"You said that Barbara was dead. Was she working here when she died?" I asked. I saw no reason not to get straight to the point.

There was a long pause filled only by static.

Finally, he said, "Yes, she was."

"What happened?"

Another pause.

"She was killed in a hit-and-run."

"Was there an investigation?"

"Barely. All that the witnesses gave us was that it was a black car, which is not much to go on."

For a moment, I wished that I had been there. I could probably have given them the make, model, year, and license plate. That was closely followed by the thought that if I had been there, it might have been me getting run down.

"The local cops were quick to hand it over to the military police, who did nothing with it either," continued Morgan. "Neither of them knew she was anything more than an administrative assistant, so they had no reason to regard her death as suspicious."

"What about you? I noticed that you didn't describe it as a 'hit-and-run accident.' I assume that was not a casual oversight."

Morgan sighed heavily. "I don't believe it was an accident. I believe she was targeted. However, my director Wardour disagrees. And he says that with no real evidence it was anything more than a coincidence, we can't have the security services investigate without risking unwanted attention."

I hated coincidences. I tried my best to keep my voice calm and level. "This would have been useful information to have before I agreed to this assignment, don't you think?"

"I wanted to tell you, honestly, but my superiors nixed it. They were afraid it would scare you off."

"Well, yes, that's rather the point, isn't it?" I said, making no effort to keep the snarky tone out of my voice. "And you realize I now feel like I'm the one who got Barbara killed?"

"Please don't say that," said Morgan. "Nobody forced her to take the assignment. She didn't even know you'd turned it down. If anybody should feel responsible, it's me for putting her into a situation she wasn't qualified for. And I do feel responsible, by the way. This is not what I signed up for either. I'm an analyst, not a handler for field agents."

"Well, it's nice to know you have some sort of a conscience."

"Look, we will all understand if you want to bail out."

"You know I can't do that. This isn't just an espionage case now; it's also a murder case. And Barbara was a colleague and a friend. But I do have a question and a condition."

"What's the question?" he asked.

"Did Barbara slip up or was she betrayed? Who knew about her?"

"In the bureau, my chain of command knew about the plan, but only Wardour and I knew her identity. Everything about this case is kept under lock and key in my safe. On base, only Hathaway knows about the investigation. And the condition?"

"I want Joy read in. I need to have somebody I trust completely that I can call and talk through my thoughts with."

He sighed heavily, and for a few seconds, the line was silent apart from static again.

"I can arrange that, assuming she has no security issues in her background. We'll set up the same secure phone protocol with her. It might take a week for the security clearance."

"That's not good enough," I told him, my voice raised and clipped. "I need her right now. I know you have your processes, but if you trust me, you trust her. Figure it out." It was an unusual tone for me, but I was channeling a lot of anger. Anger over Barbara, and anger over the information that had been withheld from me.

"Very well. I'll try to get it done in 48 hours. No guarantees."

"And I'll try not to get killed in the meantime," I said drily.

Chapter Five

Over drinks and cigarettes (my usual Kools, Malboro for her), Ali shared her story. She had escaped from Poland to the US just ahead of the Nazis. Thanks to the sponsorship of cousins here, she had managed to get in at a time when a lot of refugees were being turned away. Her brother, a fighter pilot, had gotten out after the fall of Poland, escaping through Romania, and eventually making his way to England. He had flown with the RAF and stayed in England after the war, not wanting to return to a country under Soviet occupation.

"Your English is excellent," I said.

"Thank you. It is my third language," she replied.

"What's your second?" I asked, curious.

"German. It helped me get this assignment, but I prefer not to speak it if I can avoid it. It is the language of the enemy, and I do not want the Germans to think they can be friends with me."

"I'm surprised you can bear working this close to Nazis," I said.

"It is not a happy place, but for me, the most important thing now is to oppose Stalin. Most people here do not know what went on in Poland under the Soviets, or what is still going on now. Everybody wanted to pretend that Uncle Joe was a good guy, as long as he was fighting against Hitler. They forget he invaded Poland. My homeland is an occupied country now, just as it was in 1939." Her voice was becoming increasingly intense and excited "For me, the Russians should be in Nuremberg alongside the Nazis. The sooner Stalin is brought down, the better it will be for everybody—even for the Russians themselves. This position feels like the most I can give to that objective, even if I am just typing and filing. So I hold my nose and put up with the Germans and occasionally remind them that they lost."

I laughed at that, and she smiled too. I think she felt better to have gotten that rant out of her system. "Honestly, I feel much the same about these Germans. Once they've given up everything they know, they should all go to prison."

"I will drink to that," she said.

We finished our drinks and headed over to the mess hall.

"Do you want to sit with Caroline again?" Ali asked me as we passed through the door to the mess.

"If it's not a social *faux-pas*, I'd like to meet some more people. As long as I won't be offending Caroline and her circle. I don't need to make enemies on my second day."

"Do not worry about that," Ali replied. "Caroline will decide you are a friend one day, and then just as quickly decide you are an enemy, and you will never know why. Eating dinner with her again might be considered a presumption, or not eating with her might be rude. And her little clique will go along with whatever she dictates."

"Oh good grief, it's worse than high school!" I exclaimed.

"I know nothing of American high school," said Ali. "But if it is ruled by girls like Caroline, I am grateful for that."

A man in officer's uniform was waving at us, and Ali led us over to his table. Sitting with him was a civilian in an unbuttoned white lab coat over a well-worn tweed jacket. Ali introduced him as Doctor William Reardon.

"C-c-call me Bill," he stuttered, blushing. He was a beanpole of a man, his face narrow and dominated by a large nose.

The officer introduced himself as Lieutenant Lewis. "Ted to my friends," he said, standing and reaching across the table to shake my hand. His shake was firm and lingered a little longer than completely necessary. He was broad-shouldered, tall enough, and had a wide smile and easy laugh. He struck me as the kind of man who enjoyed an easy popularity with girls, and knew it. In other words, he was not remotely my type, even if I didn't already have a steady.

I asked Bill what he was working on. He immediately launched into an enthusiastic and technical explanation accompanied by complicated hand gestures that meant almost nothing to me, except that the words "fuel inlet" came up quite a lot. Any signs of awkwardness disappeared along with his stutter as he delivered what was rapidly turning into a lecture. He pushed his heavy square-framed glasses up his nose at least once a minute. By the time he wound down, his food was cold and the rest of us had finished eating.

"Well, you did ask," said Ted, smiling again. "Bill thinks he's really onto something important, but the Germans don't give him any respect. They're hung up on a different approach they were working on before the war ended."

"And what about you, Ted?" I asked.

"Oh, nothing very exciting. Administrative this-and-that for the engine tests. Making sure Bill and the others get the resources they need. That sort of thing."

I immediately decided there was more to Ted than he was letting on. The way he had waved off his chance to talk about his job seemed somehow off to me. In my experience, men like Ted were always happy to talk about themselves.

"So what are doing tonight?" he asked. "Coming over to the club for a drink?" He was leaning forward and looking me straight in the eyes, which I found profoundly uncomfortable. Was he trying to flirt with me?

"Sorry, not tonight," I told him. "I'm still getting over my journey here, so I'm planning on an early night."

With that I pushed my chair back, got up, and said my goodbyes to Bill and Ali. I wasn't going to tell Ted, but I had much more interesting plans than anything he had in mind.

Back at my room, I had some time to kill. I picked up my Steinbeck and listened to the radio until close to nine, when I judged that people would be settled in wherever they were spending the evening, and there would be few people coming back and forth from the social clubs. First, I tied a scarf to the door handle so that Caroline wouldn't interrupt me at an unfortunate moment. I changed into black pants and a black sweater. I pinned my hair up and covered it with a black knitted hat. I wouldn't be invisible, exactly, but I should be able to hide in the shadows pretty effectively. For a few moments, I thought about pulling on my parka. I would be unremarkable to anybody who saw me—apart from the fact that I was slinking around the base where I had no business being late at night. I decided that almost-invisible was better than warm.

I stepped out of our dormitory and into the darkness of the camp. Walking swiftly over to the administrative building I'd spent the day in, huddled against the cold, I didn't see another soul. I guessed everybody was at the clubs, the base's movie theater, or in their own rooms. All of them would have been a great deal warmer than I was. I was shivering severely by the time I arrived at the door, and regretted leaving behind the parka. I stepped into the shadow of the doorway and took a moment to compose myself. I pulled off my gloves and fumbled my lockpicks from my pocket. Even though I worked here, this was probably still technically breaking and entering.

It wasn't my first time.

I looked around one more time to make sure I was unobserved and listened for any footsteps. Swiftly I opened the lock, slipped inside, closed the door behind me, and turned the lock again. As unlikely as it seemed at this time of night, I did not want some overzealous security patrol walking in on me. The last time I had broken into an office like this, it had been at a movie studio. I had almost gotten myself arrested, and Joy along with me. I did not want to repeat that experience.

There were a few things I wanted to check, and number one was the mysterious black filing cabinet. Picking a typical lock is easy; it just takes practice, patience, and focus. But picking a lock and leaving no mark—that's the art. I'd acquired the skill during the war. When I was working as a code breaker, a bunch of us taught ourselves just for the challenge of it. Since then, it had come in handy several times during investigations. I opened the lock carefully, making sure not to leave any telltale scratches that would be very obvious against the black paint, then turned on my penlight. I hadn't needed it for the lock; lockpicking is all about feel.

In the top drawer, I found half a dozen thick files. I recognized Eckert's name, and a few other top Germans. I flicked quickly through a couple of files. They looked much as one would expect: Life histories, military careers, medicals, periodic security and vetting interviews. Other than seniority, there didn't seem to be much reason for them to be so secure. If I had all night, I might have read more, but I didn't expect to find anything particularly enlightening.

The second drawer was better. The names in here were Americans, both military and civilian. Mrs. Worthington had a thick file. She had been a WAC during the war, and had stayed on as a civilian when the WACs were disbanded. Hathaway had a file too, but it had exactly one page in it, a confirmation of his security clearance. No surprise. As an intelligence officer, his file would be secured away from even Mrs. Worthington's eyes. More interestingly, my new friend Lieutenant Lewis was in there. I flicked through the file and one document immediately jumped out. The cover was stamped in red "Highly Confidential C-2" and underneath it, "Retain Secure." *What did you get red-flagged for, Ted?* I wondered.

My musing was interrupted by the sound of footsteps crunching in the gravel outside. I turned off my penlight and waited for them to pass. They did not. They stopped at the door. I didn't wait to see if their owner was coming in. I pushed the drawer closed as quietly as I could, impulsively grabbing the red-flagged document. I quick-stepped to the desks and scooted underneath my desk, the one farthest from the door, praying my penlight had not been spotted through the office window.

By this time, the door was opening. As long as the intruder stayed over by the personnel files, I would be unseen, I told myself, but if he came around this side, there was a real danger he would see me.

The light did not go on. Whoever it was, he had no more right to be in here at this time of night than I did. My heart was pounding so hard in my ears that I was convinced he must be able to hear it too. I tried to keep my breathing slow and shallow.

Suddenly, I realized that I had not relocked the black cabinet. If he tried it, he would know immediately somebody had been here—or worse, still was. I lay as still as I could, gritting my teeth to ignore my cramping legs. I peered through the gap under the desk as footsteps crossed the room and stopped. All I could see was a pair of practical black Oxfords, black socks, and the cuffed bottoms of black slacks. Nothing to give me any clue as to his identity.

I tried to guess his shoe size in case that might help later. His shoes looked to be about my size, which was a seven. Fairly small feet for a man, so that was something to look out for. I was momentarily distracted by the realization that I didn't know whether men's shoe sizes used the same scale as women's. I pulled my focus back to my present predicament.

There was only the sound of his breathing for a few moments, then I heard a lock click and one of the personnel file drawers pulled open. Then there was nothing but my own heartbeat for endless seconds. The drawer closed, and the feet came around to my side of the room. Only the fact that he had his back to me kept him from discovering me. I held my breath, and tried to calm myself by guessing his leg length up to his knee height. From the creases in the back of his pants legs, I estimated 21 inches. There's a formula for estimating a person's height from their knee height—it's amazing what you pick up when you grow up in a bookstore—so I ran the numbers in my head. It came out to around five feet eight inches, a little less than average height for a man. That wasn't much help. While I calculated, he squatted down to open one of the research drawers, and after a few seconds, closed it again. It sounded like he'd borrowed a folder. It was done so swiftly, it seemed he knew exactly where to find the one he wanted.

Finally, his feet returned to the door and left. I heard the door lock behind him. I waited another minute out of caution, then eased myself out from under the desk and tried to stretch the cramp out of my legs. I wished I knew whose personnel file the mysterious intruder had been looking at. I ran my pen light over the locks, looking for tell-tale scratches, but it looked like he had been as careful with a lock pick as I was. But judging by where he had been standing when he opened the drawer, it could well have been mine. That was a scary thought. Surely, I could not have given myself away so soon? Or perhaps whoever had found Barbara out was checking into her replacement, just to be thorough. That sounded reasonable. I hoped that my cover story would hold water. Right now, though, I wanted to know what secrets Lewis was harboring. I carefully relocked the black cabinet and slipped out.

As soon I got back to my room, I changed into my nightgown and I took the opportunity to read through the Lewis file. It turned out that before the war, he had been mixed up with several Communist friends, although he had never been a card-carrying member of the Party himself. He'd been interviewed about it and had claimed that it was because the Communists were the only ones opposing Franco's fascists in Spain. That was a common enough story back then. He had promptly repudiated his former colleagues, even implicating some of them in attempts to pass secret information to the Soviets, so his interviewer had cleared him of any security risk. I assumed that the information about his past was confidential because others might not be so tolerant of a former Red, and it might be used to blackmail him. I had to also assume that Hathaway knew about Lewis's checkered past, and wondered whether that meant Lewis was under his thumb, perhaps being forced to inform on his current colleagues if he heard anything out of order. I would have to be extremely careful around him.

I put the folder under my mattress and removed the scarf from the door. I took myself to bed, my head buzzing with theories. Despite what I had learned about Barbara, I was feeling slightly less pessimistic about the investigation than I had the night before. Whatever other restrictions I was working under, I told myself, they could never take away two things: my analytical mind, and my lock picks. *Actually*, said a particularly pedantic part of my brain, *they can take away your lock picks if they find out about them.* I reminded it that I could pick some locks with just a bobby pin, so there.

It shut up, and I tried to get some sleep.

Chapter Six

Tuesday morning, I woke at six to the jarring ring of my alarm clock and slapped it into silence. My brain had not come up with anything interesting about my small-shoed man of average height while I slept. I supposed I would be spending the next few days surreptitiously glancing at men's feet.

Caroline was in her bed and had slept through my alarm. I tiptoed around the room to avoid waking her, collecting clothes and my toiletry bag, and headed for the showers. By eight o'clock, I was dressed, breakfasted, and sitting in one of the phone booths. I needed to call Morgan again, and even though it was only five in the morning for him, I expected he would be at his desk as promised. I was soon proven correct.

"Do you have something for me already?" Morgan asked. He sounded surprised to be hearing from me again so soon.

"Maybe. I need you to look up one of the officers here on base. He seems to be trying very hard to make me think he's charming but unimportant. It feels fake to me."

"Name?"

"Lieutenant Lewis. Goes by Ted, might officially be Edward."

"And this is just based on a feeling?"

"No, there's also something more solid. His personnel file has a C-2 flag. It says he was interviewed about his pre-war ties to Communists."

"I'm not going to ask how you got access to a C-2 report, although it does make me worry about base security. It sounds like a case of 'hard on the outside, soft on the inside.'"

"With his record, he must assume he'd always be under suspicion," I continued, "but it would be nice to know what else the intelligence services have on him that's not in his army file. And maybe it makes him vulnerable to blackmail, even if he has officially sworn off his Communist past."

"This disturbs me too," said Morgan. "For somebody with that flag on his record, even as only a fellow traveler, clearing him to work on a base like the TDL would require sign off from somebody pretty senior. It's certainly above my pay grade. I'll see what I can learn. It could take several days for any of the other agencies to get back to us, though. Anything else?"

"Yes. Can you pull immigration records for Alicja Barbinksi?" I asked, spelling it out for him. "In particular, who sponsored her for entry?" I wasn't sure what I was looking for, but it didn't hurt to verify her background story. After all, she was a foreigner with little history in the US, and it would be naive to simply take her at face value.

"Sure, although that may take even longer to come back."

"I'll check in again in a couple of days," I told him, and hung up.

I had plenty of time for a cigarette and another coffee before the start of another day of tedious filing. Perhaps I shouldn't have mentioned Ali's name to Morgan. I didn't have any real reason to doubt her, and I hoped merely asking about her would not endanger her security clearance.

The day passed slowly, and inevitably Ali and I went for a drink afterwards, then to dinner. We sat with more strangers and listened to them gossip. After we finished, we went back to the officers' club, hoping for better conversation. I noticed Caroline there, chatting with some lieutenant, and decided not to interrupt. By nine, I'd had enough. I hadn't heard anything nearly as interesting as what I knew about Ted, and I was tired of smiling politely while men talked about themselves. I made my excuses to Ali and left to spend the rest of the evening with the radio and a good book. On my way out, I noticed that Caroline had ditched the lieutenant for a captain.

Caroline was not back by the time I went to bed. I hoped she wouldn't wake me when she came in.

I slept badly again, and Wednesday morning came far too soon. After a minute of stretching and yawning, I registered that Caroline was not in her bed, which did not look slept in. Either she had risen before me and been very quiet about it, or she had spent the night elsewhere, possibly with a scarf of her own tied to the door handle. Fraternization, as it was euphemistically known on base, was not forbidden, unless it "interfered with military discipline." I didn't know what exactly fell under that clause, but I imagined it was a warning against sleeping with somebody else's wife or husband, among other things.

Ali was in before me that morning, already at work with the research reports. I continued to work through the personnel records backlog, taking every opportunity to look for anything out of the ordinary. It looked like Ali hadn't even touched them since Barbara's departure. Mrs. Worthington gave no indication that she was aware that two intruders had been in the office overnight, let alone that her precious black cabinet had been interfered with. That reminded me, eventually I was going to have to find a way to return the document I had borrowed. Perhaps I could negotiate something with Hathaway.

We were interrupted around eleven by an orderly. He knocked hesitantly on Mrs. Worthington's door, waited for a summons, and then stepped inside. The brief conversation behind her door was inaudible. When he stepped out, he spoke to Ali.

"Miss Babinski, please come with me. This won't take very long."

Ali and I exchanged glances and shrugs. She followed the orderly outside and I returned to my filing, my mind running at a hundred miles an hour generating scenarios, few of which did not involve me going to military prison.

About twenty minutes later, the orderly returned with Ali in tow. She looked distraught, her eyes red and puffy as if she had been crying. I wanted to ask her what was going on, but she gave me the smallest shake of the head.

"You next please, Miss Stone," said the orderly, and I followed him obediently. Frankly, I was so curious to know what was going on I would have followed him even without an invitation.

We walked in silence for a few minutes and entered another of the indistinguishable low concrete block buildings that made up most of the base, each identified by letters, numbers, and impenetrable military abbreviations. There was a small reception area set up in front, and the secretary behind the desk waved me through. The orderly walked me up to a door with 'Capt. Hathaway' on the nameplate, knocked, and left me to it.

I sat down at the desk across from Hathaway. He was average height, with a round, ruddy face that suggested a drinking man, and circular wireframe glasses. Unfortunately, I couldn't see his feet without ducking under the desk, which I thought would have been awkward. He looked at me for longer than felt I comfortable with, tapping a pencil annoyingly on the desk. I'm not good at reading faces, but even to me, he looked stressed.

"Miss Stone," he finally said, "I know who you are, of course, and why you're here. This is not about that."

"That's a relief," I replied. "I'd hate to think I'd done something to attract attention already."

"I'm also not going to ask how your investigation is going."

"Also a relief, since I wouldn't tell you if you did."

"Let me get to the point. Caroline was attacked last night."

"Oh my gosh!" I exclaimed, leaning forward. "Is it bad?"

"She's in the medical center. Cuts, bruises, one cracked rib. A bump on the head, possibly when she was knocked down. When she's rested up a little, she'll be transferred to the hospital in town. Physically, she'll be uncomfortable for a few days, no more than that, we hope."

"And mentally?"

"Harder to say. It happened right here on the base, so you can imagine she might well be scared for her safety until we find who did this. We've never had anything like this before."

"You're leading the investigation, I take it."

"Yes. I'm interviewing everybody in her immediate circle, trying to narrow down her movements last night. If I don't get anywhere, I'll have to cast a wider net."

"What time period are you looking at?" I asked. My brain had immediately clicked into investigator mode.

"She was found around midnight, behind one of the admin buildings, by a patrol. And she was in the officers' club up until nine at least. So that leaves three hours unaccounted for."

"Unfortunately, I'm going to be useless, I'm afraid. I left the club around nine and she was still there, talking to a captain. I don't know his name. I noticed she wasn't in by the time I went to bed, but I just assumed she was still out drinking." I wondered to myself if there could be any possible link between the attack and my investigation. I couldn't think of any way to connect the two, but it seemed like too much coincidence for my taste, and I didn't want to discount it entirely. And I didn't want to mention the thought to Hathaway either. I saw no reason to share my nocturnal burglary with him until I knew a great deal more about who was trustworthy and who was not.

"Honestly, this feels more like your field than military security," sighed Hathaway. "Any ideas?"

"Has she been able to tell you anything herself?"

"Nothing, really. She said that the whole evening is largely a blank between going to the club and waking up this morning. She doesn't even remember leaving the club. I guess that can happen with a blow to the head."

"Any thoughts about motive?" I asked.

He shrugged. "None at all. She wasn't robbed, and she wasn't… you know…". He tailed off awkwardly, blushing and staring at his shoes.

"Sexually assaulted?" I filled in for him. This really was out of his comfort zone in every way. "Well, if it were my investigation, I would widen the interviews immediately, while memories are still fresh. Find out who was in the club while she was there, who she was with, whether anybody seemed upset or angry, even if it wasn't somebody she spoke to."

"Why?" he asked, creasing his forehead.

"A jealous ex-boyfriend or would-be boyfriend might have been upset about her talking to somebody he saw as a rival. Ask the girls in her circle if she recently broke off a relationship with someone. She also mentioned to me that some of the hardline Germans had been trying to attach themselves to her, so that's possible."

"Okay, that's good. Anything else?"

"I assume you've already verified that she left alone? But you also want to ask if anybody left right after her, or even shortly before her. It would be a stupid thing for somebody to do if they were planning to jump her, but people often do stupid things. Especially jealous men."

Hathaway was scribbling furiously in his notepad.

"Thank you," he said. "I owe you a drink, at the very least. Like I said, this is not what I was trained for."

"Isn't there anybody else that can help?"

"Not really. In theory, there are the MPs, but they aren't investigators either. They do their thinking with their batons and boots. And I don't want to involve CID unless I really have to. I don't want them clumsily stomping around your investigation."

CID was the Army's Criminal Investigation Division, and in theory, they would have jurisdiction if the assault on Caroline was unrelated to Hathaway's counterintelligence responsibilities. Did that mean Hathaway had suspicions? Or was he just being territorial? Pragmatically, though, I didn't want CID butting in either.

"I appreciate that," I said. "It might scare our spy and make him go to ground for who knows how long."

I felt conflicted. Part of me wanted to treat Caroline's assault as a case and jump in with both feet. But as angry as I was about what had happened to her, I could not afford to get dragged into this business. If I started acting obviously like an investigator, it would attract a lot of questions, and almost certainly blow my cover. Rationally, I had done all I could for now.

"If I think of anything else useful, I'll let you know," I said. "But you'll need to come up with a reason for us to meet that doesn't draw attention to me."

He nodded. I pushed my chair back and got up. "I'd better get back. You don't want my interview to be suspiciously longer than anybody else's," I said.

"You think of every detail, don't you?" he replied.

Leaving Hathaway's office, I saw that the orderly was in the reception area with one of the girls I had sat with at Caroline's table on my first night. I didn't remember her name, and made a mental note—yet again—to figure out how to get better at that. The orderly decided that I didn't need an escort back to my office, and simply nodded to me as I left.

As I walked back to the office, I thought ruefully that this whole business would be a lot easier if they just gave me Hathaway's job. Both my investigation and his case. Approaching the door, I recalled how distraught Ali had looked when she returned, and realized that I ought to show some sort of distress over Caroline, even though my feelings were strictly anger and a desire for justice. On an objective level, what had happened to her was awful, but I didn't know her or like her well enough to feel entitled to be sad or distraught on her behalf. Apparently, that sort of reaction made me cold, or so I had been told. I rubbed my eyes and my eyelids as hard as I dared, trying to make them red, and hoped that would pass for emotion.

CHAPTER SEVEN

On Wednesday after work, I called Morgan yet again. I doubted he had expected this much contact as soon as my feet hit the ground. He confirmed that I was clear to talk to Joy. I was hugely relieved. I had worried that he might uncover that Joy was a lesbian, a disclosure she had shared with me a few months previously. The army had banned gay men from service for decades, and the WACs had officially excluded lesbians—and unofficially, anybody who was even remotely suspected of possibly being a lesbian—in 1944, but I had no idea where the various intelligence services stood. It was even possible that some priggish official might deem it disqualifying, even if there was no official policy. Morgan either didn't know or didn't care. I hung up and immediately contacted Joy.

"Hey kid, how's it going?" she asked. She was only two years older than me, but I had given up trying to get her to stop calling me 'kid.'

"Okay. How was the clearance process?" I replied.

"Awful. Like a month's worth of paperwork in two days. And they asked some very personal questions about my known associates, if you know what I mean."

"Sorry you had to go through that. But I can't tell you how glad I am to have you on the inside. Let me bring you up to speed with what I know." I shared the contacts and conversations I'd had so far as concisely as I could.

"So who do you like for it? Do you trust Hathaway?"

"It seems unlikely Hathaway would be stealing documents himself, but he'd be well placed to provide cover for whoever the spy is, should he be so inclined. But honestly, I get the impression that he's not bright enough for that sort of thing. And I don't yet know of any motive for him to do so."

"Is Lewis a possibility?" asked Joy.

"Possible, not probable, I would say. With his record, he would expect to be under strict scrutiny, and the consequences would be severe. But I do feel like he's playing the harmless goof with me, which worries me."

"Any progress on the intruder from your little break-in?"

"No," I sighed. "It shouldn't be this hard to spot a man with small feet on an army base."

"Or," said Joy thoughtfully, "a woman with average feet."

"He was wearing black dress pants and Oxfords," I pointed out.

"I know lots of women who dress like that," replied Joy. "I've even dated a couple."

I realized that I had been harboring a really dumb assumption, which made me more than a little mad at myself. That was not like me at all, to discount what women were capable of.

"Damn, I completely overlooked that possibility. But why would she be dressed that way for a break-in?"

"So that if she was seen in the dark, she'd be taken for a man? Or if she left footprints, they wouldn't obviously be a woman's?" suggested Joy.

"Yes, that's smart," I said slowly. "So we'd be looking for a woman who takes a size seven shoe," I said, doing the math in my head again, since the formula was different for women, "and she'd be about five feet six. That doesn't narrow things down much, but at least I'm looking at the right people's feet now."

"Well, that's something. What about the scientists?"

"It would be awfully risky for any of the Germans, given what would happen to them if they were caught. Being sent back to Germany is probably a death sentence for some of them, and being turned over to the Russians might be worse. But I suppose it's possible and I'm certainly not ruling them out. Getting close to them is going to be difficult, though, not to mention unpleasant." I really did not want to encourage any thoughts they might have that I would be willing to fraternize with them any more than duty required.

"I have an idea here," said Joy. "You should get in with the motor pool drivers. People in the back of a car are amazingly indiscreet. They forget their driver is listening to every word they say. I'll bet they have lots to say about the Germans, and none of it will be complimentary."

It was true. As a former cabbie, Joy had some amazing stories of her own.

"They are likely to have a lot of scuttlebutt about everybody else on base, too," she continued. "All the drivers I know are total gossips. It's practically a currency for them. If you're looking for somebody with money problems, or somebody splashing too much around, for that matter, they'll know. And if somebody has a sex scandal, they'll be all over that. You'll need some story of your own to trade, though."

"Fact or rumor?" I asked.

"Either. As long as it's something juicy."

I would have to give that some thought. I hated the idea of spreading gossip about somebody, especially if it wasn't true. Or maybe even more so if it was.

"Or," she added, "you could try flirting with them."

I was about to protest that I had no idea how to flirt, before realizing that she knew that perfectly well. She was teasing me. I could picture the smirk on her face as she waited for me to take the bait. It had only been a handful of days, but I already missed our banter.

She was right about one thing, though. I had been putting off talking to the enlisted men. I felt that I had very little common ground with them. I wished I had Joy here to do it for me, but I was just going to have to get over my awkwardness. Maybe if I pretended to myself that I was just chatting with the cabbies at Jack's, that would help.

"Tomorrow, then. I'll go to the enlisted men's bar and see what I can pick up." Saying it out loud made it feel like a promise to Joy, and that would keep me from giving myself an excuse to back out.

"What about the other Americans?"

"Nobody stands out yet, but I'm more suspicious of them than of the Germans, honestly. There's plenty of people who were sympathetic towards Russia in the thirties, and not all of them were card-carrying party members or known to the FBI. Some of them were turned off when the truth started to come out about Stalin's regime, but others somehow managed to justify it to themselves."

"Let's not assume it has to be political, though. There's always sex and money."

"Yes, I've thought that too."

"Have you thought about somebody doing it for attention?"

"What do you mean?" I asked, feeling my face scrunch in confusion.

"Somebody who feels they aren't appreciated, or their work is undervalued. Or somebody who doesn't fit in with his own people. Maybe they don't come from a good enough family for the others, that kind of thing, even though their work is good. A little flattery might turn their head."

"Or someone might be worried they don't come from a good enough university," I added, pensively. "The Germans do seem to have constructed their own class system here. But would that be enough for somebody to risk treason?"

Joy laughed. "You really don't get people, do you? People will do some really dumb things to feel wanted."

"Thanks, that's a good insight. Anything else?"

"One last thing. I hate to ask this," said Joy, "but what about Morgan himself? Trustworthy?"

I sighed and shrugged. "I think we have to trust him, otherwise we're going to get nowhere. After all, he did bring us in to solve this thing."

"Unless he thinks we're terrible detectives, and he's just covering his ass with his bosses by looking like he's doing something," said Joy.

I hoped Joy was joking. I often couldn't tell.

At dinner, I joined Ali and a couple of other girls from Caroline's clique. There were only two topics of gossip at the table. At first, they wanted to speculate about what had happened to Caroline, but in the absence of any solid facts, that was soon exhausted. Almost guiltily, chatter turned to the upcoming dance on Saturday in celebration of Valentine's Day. There had been some talk of postponing it in the wake of what had happened to Caroline, but the decision from the base commander was that it would be a morale boost and help to "normalize" life at the base again.

Apparently, a real band would be making an appearance instead of the usual army band, with the promise that there'd be dancing to musicians who could actually keep a beat. The girls were soon debating dresses and shoes.

Ali looked at me plaintively. "I do not have pretty shoes to wear with my dress. My shoes are so dull," she said.

"What size do you wear?" I asked.

"Seven. Why?" she replied.

"I have a pair I could lend you. Come along with me after dinner and we'll pick something out."

I had plenty of ridiculously nice shoes, and I'd brought three pairs with me. Ginnie passed hers down to me when she was done with them, often insisting that they were hopelessly unfashionable as soon as they were just one season old. I was more than glad to have them: When you like dancing as much as I do, you'll go through shoes pretty quickly. And they were my one real concession to caring more than was professionally needed about my appearance. I also had a very practical pair of ankle boots from Ginnie, which I was really learning to love in Dayton's cold and rain. The rain here was less reliable than in LA, but heavier, colder, and somehow murkier.

Ali walked back with me after dinner, and I tried to get her to open up a little about her personal life. I asked if there was anybody in particular she hoped to dance with, but she just shook her head and stared at her feet. I couldn't blame her for not being forthcoming. If our positions were reversed, I would probably have reacted the same way. After she left clutching a pair of black slingback pumps that she said would be perfect with her one good dress, I tied a scarf around the door handle and pulled it closed. I had turned down her offer of a drink. I had much thinking to do.

I pulled my notebook out of my purse and started to write down everything I knew. Sometimes this helped me unlock my thoughts. I jotted down names and wrote "Means? Motive? Opportunity?" underneath, with checkmarks against some of them. I drew circles and joined them with lines. I erased things. I put my pencil down and slammed my book shut in frustration. I felt like I was flailing.

Suddenly, I realized that I had not mentioned Ali to Joy, not even as the closest thing to a friend I had here. Was I subconsciously shielding her because I thought we were alike? But... she was the right height and had the right shoe size to be the intruder in the office. And of course she had keys to the filing cabinets, so she wouldn't have had to pick their locks. I had no idea whether she could have picked the door lock, or if she even had a duplicate key somehow. In addition, whoever was in the office that night knew exactly what they were looking for and went straight to it. Who else knew the arrangement of the files that well? Was that why she was keeping the research files to herself and leaving the personnel files to me?

Worst of all, it struck me that she would have had much more opportunity to observe Barbara than would anybody else on base. If Barbara had slipped and given herself away, chances were that it would have been Ali who noticed. Or it could have been the other way around: Barbara might have caught Ali doing something suspicious. Was it conceivable that Ali was responsible for Barbara's death? And did that mean she had a collaborator, somebody with ready access to a car?

Ali had all the means and opportunity, but I could think of no motive—quite the reverse, in fact. She had every reason to hate the Soviets, and she had sounded passionate when she talked about her opposition to Stalin. And objectively, the narrative I was spinning around Ali was based entirely on circumstantial evidence, including an estimated shoe size that probably described one in three of the women here. Not exactly a Cinderella's glass slipper level of exclusivity. In fact, somebody looking at this case from the outside could tell just as good a narrative about me. And I had definitely stolen a confidential document.

With all that buzzing in my brain, sleep did not come easily.

On Thursday, I did my best to stick to my routine, and not give away any of my suspicions to Ali. That was not the only thing making me tense and anxious, though. I was getting increasingly frustrated at the shackles on my investigation, my inability to question anybody straightforwardly, or even take time away from my day job without attracting attention. At first, I had thought having free access to the personnel records was going to be useful, but it was turning out to be a tedious time sink. On top of all that, pretending to be somebody else was also taking a toll on me. Working undercover had never come naturally to me, and this was by far the longest I had ever had to do it for. The constant vigilance it required was wearing, and I felt sure my awkward self-consciousness must be obvious to any observer. I kept coming back to the thought that they should have just given me Hathaway's job. A couple of years ago, that would have been a real possibility. Not now, though. All those gains I thought women had made during the war were, it seemed, slowly but unrelentingly being eroded.

I tried to focus my thoughts on Saturday and the upcoming Valentine's dance, thinking about how I might exploit it. I wondered if I could make some excuse and leave the party early. It would be the perfect time to be doing a little breaking and entering while everybody else was distracted. I'd like to check out Ted Lewis's room. I wanted to know more about him. And I guessed it wouldn't hurt to see whether Ali had a pair of black Oxfords stashed in the back of her cupboard. It was tempting, but with so few women on the base, my absence would be too conspicuous. I told myself I should treat it as a chance to glean some intelligence from people, perhaps while they had their guards down a little.

And at least there would be dancing. I deserved that, if only for one evening.

Before Saturday could come, however, the investigation had one more twist to throw at me. Thursday evening, I finished up work promptly at five, told Ali I would probably see her before dinner at the officer's club, and headed back to my room for a little rest. Stepping inside, my foot slipped away from under me. I grabbed for the door jamb and barely kept myself upright. Looking down I saw the cause. Somebody had pushed an envelope under my door. I had stepped on it, sending it skidding across the room, and almost sending myself tumbling.

I picked up the envelope and examined it. *Miss Stone* was typed across the front, with nothing on the back. Not helpful. I opened the envelope and pulled out a Valentine's card. It had a very generic design with red roses on a white background—the kind you might find in any Hallmark rack. I had no idea who I might have given the idea to that I was romantically interested. Mind you, that was not unusual for me. I had not realized that my current boyfriend was at all interested until Joy hit me over the head with it, metaphorically speaking.

The typed name on the outside of the envelope struck me as rather formal for a Valentine's card, but it would help the sender to remain anonymous, I supposed. Wasn't that the tradition with these things? I had very little personal experience to go on here.

I opened it. Inside there was an equally generic printed message, "Be my Valentine!", and below it, in blocky capitals, two words:

TAKE CARE

What was that supposed to mean? As an expression of affection, it seemed quite tepid. Was it a warning? A subtle threat? It wasn't the first time I'd received an unhelpfully obscure, anonymous message, and the previous time had led to blackmail, kidnapping, and murder before all was said and done. I really wished people would be clearer with their threats. It would make things a lot simpler for both of us.

I found Ali at the club and bought her a vodka. I lit a Kool and took a deep draw, hoping it would settle my nerves which, I realized, were jangling from the implications of the anonymous card. Neither one of us felt particularly conversational, it turned out, and we smoked and drank in uneasy silence before heading over for dinner. We listened to a couple of the other girls compare opinions on dresses, shoes, and Perry Como while we ate. I hurried through my meal, excused myself, and stood to leave.

"Are you going back to the officer's club?" Ali asked. "I think I want one more drink."

"I'm going to check out the enlisted men's club tonight. I feel like a change of pace."

Ali screwed up her face. "Ugh. Not for me. I went there once only, and it was too loud and rough. And the talk of the men was very crude. I did not enjoy."

That didn't sound like my idea of fun either, but I was determined to go through with it. Joy's advice about the drivers was on the nose. I would just have to find my moxie, as Joy would tell me if she were here.

I paused at the door to the club. I told myself not to slip into what Joy called my bookstore voice, something I tended to do with strangers and when I was anxious about the impression I was making. I reminded myself to imagine I was talking to our cabbie friends at Jack's. I stepped inside. Conversation did not stop. The whole room did not stare at me. I did not die from self-consciousness.

As I walked over to the bar, I formed my first impressions. The place seemed a bit louder and a bit smokier than the officers' club, but not nearly as bad as Ali had set me up to expect. The furniture was a little cruder, the floor a little dirtier, but nothing compared to Jack's. A group of about a dozen men sat on benches along both sides of a long table, beers in front of them, laughing and joking. One of them stood up as I passed and fell in step alongside me.

"Evening, miss," he said, touching his fingers to his forehead in a gesture somewhere between a salute and a tip of the cap he wasn't wearing. "Haven't seen you in here before. Maybe I can buy you your first drink?"

My first instinct was to say no, but I was channeling Joy tonight, and I wanted to seem welcoming, not standoff-ish.

"Thanks, soldier," I said. "I'm Dot, by the way."

"Ricky," he replied.

I turned to the barman. "Rye, please. Neat. Top shelf."

Ricky might have raised his eyebrows at my order, but he didn't say anything. I had been told before it wasn't a very ladylike drink, but not by anybody I was still talking to.

"Come and join us," he said, indicating his table. "We don't bite, and we're very respectful to ladies." I followed him over and his friends scooted along the bench so that I could sit next to him on the end.

"Cigarette?" he said, offering me his deck of Camels.

"Thanks, but I prefer my own," I replied, popping a Kool into my mouth. He lit it for me before lighting his own.

"Everybody, this is Dot," he announced. They went around the table and introduced themselves. I made my best effort to remember names, and I thought I got a couple.

"I'm going to apologize right now," I said. "I'm terrible at names, so you're probably all going to have to do that at least three more times. It doesn't mean I don't like you."

That got a small laugh, to my surprise. *Maybe I can do this*, I thought to myself.

"You new on base?" asked Ricky.

I nodded. "My first week," I said. "I've been drinking at the officers' club up till now."

"And you're tired of them already?" said the man across from me. Tommy, maybe?

The table laughed again and I joined in.

"Got a boyfriend?" asked a man down the end of the table.

"Yes. He's a homicide detective."

A few of them exchanged looks that I hoped meant that even if they weren't sure they believed me, they didn't want to find out the hard way.

"So what do you all do?" I asked.

"Drivers," said maybe-Tommy. "Motor pool. Truck drivers, mostly. And chauffeurs to the officers, and anybody else who manages to swing a vehicle requisition. And when the cars break, we fix them too."

Jackpot on my first try, I thought. I had caught a lucky break in my investigation.

"I bet you guys have some great stories," I said. "Back home, I'm friends with some cabbies, and they tell me that people completely forget that there's a driver up front who can hear everything."

"We sure do," smirked the man next to Tommy, "but you're going to have to give us a story in return."

"I can do that," I said, smiling. Over dinner, I had figured out what I was going to share with them. And happily, it didn't involve spreading gossip about anybody else.

"Okay, well, a couple of days ago, I was driving one of the old krauts into town—"

"Which one?" I asked, then realized from his look that I shouldn't interrupt.

"I don't know, I don't pay much attention to their names. Shaffer? Shiffer? Something like that. Anyway, he's got that Polish girl riding in the back with him. Remember her, what's her name?" he asked the rest of the table.

"Ali" and "Babinski" came overlapping replies.

"She came here once, but I guess she likes officers better," said a voice from the end of the table. There was a certain leer to the way he said it, but I decided to bite my tongue and let it pass.

"Anyway, she and the kraut are going at it like nobody's business, shouting and waving their hands. The kraut looked really angry, red in the face, and she was giving as good as she got. Meanwhile, the MP sitting next to me, their escort, he's completely stony-faced. Not his problem unless it gets physical, I guess. This went on for ten minutes, and then they didn't talk to each other the whole rest of the way there, or on the way back."

"Wow, what were they arguing about?" I asked.

"Beats me. The whole thing was in German, and the only thing I picked up when I was over there was how to order a beer."

"Not even how to pick up a fraulein?" I asked. I immediately worried it might sound like flirting.

"The frauleins all spoke the international language of stockings and cigarettes," he replied. That got a small laugh from some of the men. Apparently, their idea of 'respectful to ladies' was not the same as mine, but I kept that thought to myself too.

"If it wasn't for the invention of nylon, half of these guys wouldn't even get dates," said Ricky. That brought laughs from everybody and blushes from several.

"Okay, your turn," he continued. "What have you got for us?"

"Well, I hope this counts," I said. "Somebody pushed a Valentine's Day card under my door while I was at work today. I have no idea who. Nobody has been obviously making eyes at me that I've noticed, or hinted I should dance with them on Saturday. Maybe you guys heard something? Or have some thoughts?"

That started them all off. It seemed like it was right in their wheelhouse, and they would probably spin up half a dozen rumors of their own before they were done. The crosstalk was impossible for me to follow, but one name seemed to come up several times.

"Did somebody say Lewis?" I asked.

Ricky shushed everybody. "Yeah, Lieutenant Lewis. He fancies himself a bit of a ladies' man. Have you met him?"

"I have," I said, "and he tried to hit on me right away." I didn't know if that was really true, but it fit the story I was telling.

"You better watch that guy," said another voice. "He buys Valentine's Cards by the dozen."

That got the table laughing again. It seemed to be the kind of group that laughed easily with each other.

"Hey, do you guys mind if I stick around a while if I buy a round?" I asked.

"A dame buying the drinks? That's a new one on me," said maybe-Tommy, "but I ain't got no objections."

I bit down my urge to correct his double negative.

"I'll help you carry," said Ricky.

This was going about as well as I could have hoped. I didn't know how long I could stave off my inherent dislike of groups—when it comes over me, it's like a curtain coming down, giving me my cue to get off stage—but for now, I was feeling okay. Maybe I would get some more intel before the evening was over. Perhaps something of Joy was rubbing off on me.

I finally left around nine, fending off various offers to walk me back to my dorm. I'd heard a lot more stories, many of them entertaining, but none of them particularly useful. I had a lot to think about, most of all, I needed to decide whether I was letting my friendship with Ali blur my objectivity.

CHAPTER EIGHT

Friday was another fruitless day in the office. Ali still had me on personnel records, and kept the research notes to herself. *But the choice could be completely innocent, a sensible division of the work into two specializations,* I told myself. *Or it could be a good way to know where everything is, so she could come back for the good stuff when I wasn't around.*

I was still frustrated by how little I could do, and by how few conversations I could risk without seeming suspicious. Maybe I should break in somewhere, just to feel like I was doing something productive. I had a momentary urge to tie Mrs. Worthington to a chair and beat a confession out of her, just so I could go home.

When five o'clock came around, I told Ali I was going to freshen up back at my dorm, and promised to meet her at the club. I took my time, washing my face and reapplying makeup, changing out of my shoes and into my boots—rain was forecast again—and pulling on a warm cardigan and my raincoat against the wind. As much as anything, I needed to clear my head of the dull fog of filing.

As I approached the club, I heard raised voices. It sounded like German, but I couldn't make anything out over the wind. I stepped closer. The voices were coming from around the side of the building. I crept up to the corner where I could hear more. Definitely German.

The voice shouting now was male: *"You need to do as I tell you. This is not good enough! You know what will happen if you don't!"*

The reply came from a woman. And not just any woman. It was Ali. *"Stop it! I just want you to leave me alone!"*

That was enough for me. I stepped around the corner. Ali looked close to tears and the man was ruddy with anger. She was trapped against the wall, and he was gripping her by the wrist as she struggled to free herself. He was a hefty man, only about five feet eight, but very heavy set. His face was jowly and what little hair he had was in a close military-style crop. He was on the verge of shouting at her again when he realized I was there.

"Is everything okay, Ali?" I said, not taking my eyes off of him.

"What do you want? Don't interfere!" he shouted at me, as angrily as he had been speaking to Ali, his jowls bouncing in time with his words.

"I heard shouting, and after what happened to Caroline, I was worried," I said. I made an effort to keep my voice calm.

He dropped Ali's wrist, turned to face me, and stepped in close. I think he was trying to intimidate me. It wasn't working. I'd been intimidated by experts. Literally. On our first case, Joy and I had run into a mobster called Accardo, and he had been extremely good at it. The biggest threat this guy offered was that he might fall over and land on me.

"This is none of your business. Stay out of it!" he said, slightly less confident now.

I looked him straight in the eye. "Did he touch you, Ali? Do we need to make a report to the MPs?"

He took a moment to think about that, then stepped back, his face draining from red to white. I thought it might be dawning on him how much trouble he could be in, and what the consequences might be. One woman complaining about him could easily be dismissed as 'he said, she said.' Two could not be waved off so easily.

I glanced quickly at Ali before returning my eyes to the German's. Ali was rubbing her wrist and staring down at the ground.

"Please, no MPs. No report," she said quietly.

The German pushed past me, bumping my shoulder, and stomped off into the twilight.

"Let's get you a drink," I said.

Ali nodded.

I took her elbow, which, for me, was an expression of deep concern. I didn't like to touch other people, nor be touched. But I thought that Ali needed it right then. I just hoped she didn't take it as an invitation to hug me later.

"Rye for me, vodka for her," I told the barman. I looked at Ali, and saw she was even paler than usual, and her fingers were trembling. "Make hers a double," I added. She was trying to light a Marlboro, but her hands were shaking too much. I lit it for her, then lit my own. With a gentle hand on her arm, I guided her to a table.

"What was that about?" I asked her.

She shook her head. "Nothing. He does not like my work, that is all."

"He seemed quite passionate about it," I replied.

"He is just a very angry, stupid man," she said and took a swig of her vodka. "I will be okay in a few minutes."

"What is his name?" I asked.

"You are going to report him?" she said. She looked extremely anxious, even to me. "Please no reports. It makes a lot of trouble for me."

"I promise, no reports. But I would still like to know who he is."

"He is Doctor Schäfer. He is head of a team working on aero-" She paused. "Aero-something, you know?"

"Aerodynamics?"

"Yes, thank you. Difficult word to say, difficult word to spell." She giggled a little at the end there. The vodka seemed to be kicking in, accelerated by the adrenaline.

"Please," she continued, "let us talk of more happy things. Tell me something about your life before."

It wasn't my favorite topic, but I figured it might help her to settle. I told her about losing my mother when I was young, growing up in the bookstore, and taking it over when my father died. I skipped the bit in between where I'd worked for the army as a cryptographer, breaking German codes, and filled it in with a story about spending four years at college, studying art history. I figured I'd picked up enough on the topic from the bookstore that I could bluff my way through that if challenged.

As I talked, another part of my brain was going over my encounter with Doctor Schäfer. Three things were bothering me. One, his English accent had been very good. But it was British, not American. All of the other Germans I'd heard here had very obvious German accents when they spoke English. Two, 'Schäfer' sounded an awful lot like 'Shiffer', especially when mispronounced by an American.

And three, what could it mean that he didn't like her work? Did he come by and inspect her filing when I wasn't around? The whole business seemed off, and I desperately wanted to know more about Herr Doctor Schäfer.

"Come on," I said. "Let's get some food. It'll help take your mind off things."

"It is true. When I eat here, it is hard to think about anything besides how bad the food is," she replied.

I thought she was probably joking, but I often struggled to tell when something was meant to be funny if it could also be literally true. I felt much the same way about jokes that I did about threats: I wished they came with clear instructions.

We finished our drinks, which seemed to have steadied Ali's nerves and unsteadied her feet, and headed for the mess hall. I was torn between propping her up now, or possibly catching her later.

We sat down at a table with a couple of the other girls. Enough people were there that I wouldn't have to carry the conversation alone, but there were not so many that it would be overwhelming. They introduced themselves as Fran and Liz, and they apparently worked in the typing pool. I quickly dismissed them—and the rest of the typing pool—as possible suspects. Obviously, the researcher's freehand notes would cross their desks, but they would have no control over what reports they were given to type up, so it would be impossible for them to target specific information. They would also have no easy way to smuggle information out, unless they had memories even more remarkable than mine. Unless, a small and annoying part of my brain suggested, the entire typing pool is in on it, including the supervisor. They could all be surreptitiously making carbon copies that they smuggle out at the end of each day. And somebody could be covering up the excess paper usage. I told my brain to shut up about that topic.

The main subject of conversation was, once again, the upcoming dance. Ali and I were mostly passive listeners.

"What will you do if one of the Germans asks you to dance?" Fran asked Liz.

"Oh, ugh," Liz replied, "especially if it's one of the old ones!"

"I bet they're all dead hoofers!" Fran giggled.

"Unless it's a slow waltz. That's all they do back in Germany." They both laughed annoyingly girlishly.

I jumped in. "I didn't realize the Germans would be invited too," I said.

"Afraid so," said Liz. "They want us to start mixing with them socially."

Fran leaned forward conspiratorially. "I heard it's all part of the plan," she stage-whispered loud enough for people two tables away to hear.

"Plan?" I asked, bemused.

"To teach them American culture and manners. They can't keep them locked up on army bases forever. Eventually, they're going to have to settle them somewhere."

Actually, 'locked up on army bases forever' sounded good to me, if prison wasn't an option.

"The neighbors are going to love that," said Liz.

"Release them into the wild," mumbled Ali, and giggled at her own witticism. Was she really that drunk on two vodkas, I wondered? Or had she been drinking before I found her? A drinking problem for somebody working in a classified research facility would be one more reason to worry about her.

And then I realized there was another question I hadn't asked. Maybe because subconsciously, I didn't want to know the answer.

"Where do the Germans go at night? I don't think I've ever seen one in the officers' club."

"They have a bar of their own, where they can go and speak German for a change and complain to each other about how their lives have turned out and how bad American beer is," said Fran. It sounded like she had seen it first hand.

"On Friday nights, they have a movie club with German films the army brought in for them," added Liz.

"Do they sit there watching *Triumph of the Will* on a loop while crying into their beer?" I asked. The others looked at me, obviously confused. Apparently that piece of propaganda wasn't as universally known as I thought. File that for future reference.

Ali had finished her food, and I thought she might be sobering up a little. Another drink at the officer's club would be a very bad idea, however much she thought she needed it.

"Let me walk you home," I told her.

She nodded agreement.

We walked back to her dorm, not far from mine, and the cold night air seemed to help her somewhat. By the time we got there, it had started to rain, stinging icy drops that felt more like pins on the skin than water. I stayed with her all the way to the door to her room. I really wanted to come inside and search the room for concealed bottles of vodka (and, yes, to check her closet for a pair of black Oxfords) but I couldn't think of any way in less awkward than offering to put her to bed, and that felt extremely awkward indeed.

I did have another plan for the evening, though. I intended to end the week the way I had started it: breaking and entering. I changed into what I was now thinking of as my burglary outfit, and after some consideration, pulled on a parka too. If I was seen out in this weather, it would attract more attention to not be wearing one. And besides, I'd learned my lesson from last time. It had been brutally bitter that night, and tonight was even colder.

Putting up my hood and folding my arms across my chest, I set out across the camp through the grid of near-identical buildings. First, a stopover at my office to look up where Schäfer's office was, then over to a research building several blocks away. A few people were out and about, but none paid any attention to me, being more concerned with scurrying to their own destinations before the cold got to them. The outer door to the building yielded quickly to my lock picks, and the inner door to Schäfer's office immediately after. I reflected that Morgan was right to be concerned about the security here.

I closed the blinds on the single small window before turning on my penlight. The office was unremarkable and filled with the same general issue cheap military furniture that was everywhere on the base. There was a desk, a chair behind it and a less comfortable one in front, a bookcase, and a filing cabinet. On the desk, there were the usual tools of office work, including empty In and Out trays. Presumably, everything was locked in the filing cabinet at night. The desk drawers didn't lock, but I checked them anyway. All I found was stationery, an internal phone directory, and a pocket German-English dictionary.

I turned my attention to the filing cabinet. It was the type with a single lock at the top that released all three drawers. In the top drawer, I found hand-written notes in a mixture of German and English. The middle drawer held typed reports, presumably for Schäfer to review and correct before they were filed in our archives. The bottom drawer was where I hit gold. Inside was a tough-looking aluminum case with heavily reinforced corners. It had two snap closures with good quality locks that looked like they were serious about their business.

But I also saw something bizarre. On each side of the case's opening, a small metal hoop was attached, and a padlock connected the two loops, preventing the case from opening, even if the two snap locks were defeated. I supposed it offered a little extra security, but confusingly, the padlock looked cheaply made and thoroughly shoddy, with ill-fitting parts. What was the point? It should be very easy to pick, probably even with a bobby pin, assuming it didn't fall apart completely in the attempt. I peeked into the lock to get some idea of which pick to try, and was surprised again. Inside the lock, I could see a piece of paper blocking the keyhole, with ink visible on it, depicting just a couple of letters.

I stood up and stared into the distance. *What was the point of a weak lock with a piece of paper inside?* I asked myself. Then it came to me: the lock couldn't be opened either with a key or with picks without punching a hole in the paper. And the paper was probably signed, so if somebody unauthorized opened it, they couldn't simply replace it. It wasn't there to make it hard to get in, it was there to show that somebody had. As a deterrent, it was more effective against me than any lock could have been. I had never encountered anything like it before. Was that a common intelligence technique, or just Schäfer being paranoid? I would have to ask Morgan about that. *What are you keeping so carefully protected, Herr Doctor Schäfer?* I wondered.

It was an intriguing puzzle, but I wasn't going to learn anything more tonight. Time to lock up and go home.

I reset the lock on the outer door, carefully put my lock picks away in the pocket of my pants, and zipped up my parka. Then my night took a severe turn for the worse.

"You! You there!" shouted a voice from the distance. "Stay right where you are!"

Why couldn't a break-in be a simple in and out, just for once? I asked myself. All I could see in the dark was two flashlights and two white helmets, so it was hard to judge the distance, but I had no doubt who it was. A military police patrol.

Perfect timing, I thought. I definitely did not want to explain myself to them. I dashed across the path and between two buildings, trying to think of a way to lose them. I could hear their running feet pounding behind me. They shouted a couple more times, but then gave that up, presumably to save their breath.

I didn't think I had any chance to outrun them. My boots were not made for running, unlike theirs. And they were in much better shape than I was. The longer this went on, the worse my chances would become. I zigzagged between buildings, heading towards the clubs and the dorms, hoping to find a group of people I could disappear into.

But I wasn't shaking them. I could see their flashlights bobbing at the end of the rows as they tracked my progress, and I guessed they could see me too. At the next intersection, I saw only one light; they had split up. I had to assume the other one was heading around to cut me off. I needed a new plan. I stopped and thought.

Then I had an idea. I shucked off my parka, relying on my black outfit to hide me better. Less visible was more important than warm right now. I tucked myself into the shadows as tight as I could, and crept up to the next corner. Crouching and peering around, I could see one flashlight off to my right, three buildings away, and the other one ahead of me, about the same distance.

I slipped to my left, ran as fast and as quietly as I could past two buildings, clinging to the shadows still, and found what I needed. This hut, like many on the base that had been thrown up quickly during the war, did not have a proper foundation. Instead, it rested on concrete block piers, spaced some six feet apart. It looked absolutely black under there.

I dropped down, rolled underneath, and crawled as far to the center as I could get. If they figured out what I'd done, and they were willing to systematically check under every building, they would almost certainly find me. My hope was that they would get bored and leave before I froze to death, my body never to be found. I lay still listening to the footsteps, then heard voices, not too close by. Maybe a couple of buildings away, where they had last seen me. Footsteps came toward me, and they were close enough now that I could make out the words.

"Looks like we lost him," one said.

"Grid search to try to flush him out?" said the other.

"Forget that," the first voice said. "Shift finishes in ten minutes. And this weather is for the birds."

"You're right. Let's check that the building he was messing with is secure, and then head for the bar."

I heard steps walking away, but stayed put for several more minutes. Hathaway had said the MPs were not recruited for their intelligence, but I had to guess that pretending to leave was a trick that might have occurred to even them.

Finally, I extricated myself, crawling and rolling, and headed back to the dorm, shivering all the way, and still sticking to the shadows. Not for fear that the MPs might still be lurking, but because being seen dressed like a burglar would raise eyebrows.

At last, I arrived back at my dorm and slipped into my room unseen. I heaved a sigh of relief. I needed a hot shower and a large slug from the bottle of rye I kept in my suitcase.

No, check that. Reverse it.

Chapter Nine

Saturday morning should have been a chance to relax, but I couldn't. I wandered restlessly from the dorm to the officers' club to the PX and back, but my mind wouldn't settle. I was deeply bothered by the case I had found in Schäfer's office and frustrated by my inability to look inside. I hated mysteries, and this one was nagging at me.

Around noon, an orderly found me in the common room of my dorm, drinking tea and trying to focus on reading. It was the same orderly who'd brought me to see Hathaway earlier in the week. It turned out he was taking me back to the same place.

Hathaway was sitting behind his desk as before, nervously fiddling with a pencil when I came in. His shoulders were tensed and his back was stiff. I took off my raincoat and sat down across from him without waiting to be asked.

"Miss Stone, I have received a disturbing report from the MPs. It seems a patrol interrupted somebody trying to break into Dr. Schäfer's office last night. I don't want to interfere with your investigation, but I am still responsible for base security. Do you know anything about that?"

"Thank you for letting me know," I said, my face a blank mask of professionalism. Working in the bookstore had provided plenty of practice at sealing my emotions away from my customers, and the same skill was very handy now. "It could very well be related to my case," I added. Technically, this was not a lie.

Hathaway stared at me for several seconds, trying to decide whether to challenge me further, I suspected. He tried a different tack. "They also found a parka, discarded on the ground not too far away," he said.

"I wonder if it could be Caroline's? Hers is not in our room, but I just assumed she'd taken it with her." Not entirely a lie.

He glared at me now. He didn't have remotely enough evidence to accuse me, and he appeared unwilling to confront me directly. It seemed he realized that if he continued on this path, I was just going to stonewall him.

"By the way," I continued, "have you made any progress on the attack on Caroline? Has she remembered anything?" I was genuinely interested, but it also seemed like a good way to redirect the conversation.

His shoulders slumped. "Nothing," he said, and tossed his pencil onto the desk where it rattled for a moment or two before coming to rest. "And she's decided not to return to the base, so I can't interview her further. Unless something remarkable breaks our way, I don't see any way to progress the investigation."

"Well, I'll keep my ears open in case I hear anything about anybody with a grudge against her."

I got up, put my coat back on, and turned for the door.

"Thanks for your help," he said. He did not sound very grateful, though.

I headed over to the officers' club. I needed to talk through my thoughts with Joy. We didn't open the office on weekends, but she had agreed that while I was here, she would be there between nine and ten in case I needed to call her. I pictured her with her feet up on the desk and a crime magazine open. I missed having her around, and not just as somebody to bounce ideas off.

"Hey, kid," she said once we connected. "Good to hear from you. It's awfully quiet around here without you."

"You have no idea how much I miss you too," I replied.

"So what's up?" she asked.

"I need to talk to you about a woman here named Ali Babinski. I should have mentioned her before. I feel like I might have been protecting her because she seemed to be a potential friend. Anyway, I need your objective take."

"Give me everything you've got."

I walked Joy through my experiences with Ali from first meeting her at dinner and observing her detachment from the conversation of Caroline and her friends, through working together for a week, socializing, the argument I'd overheard between her and Schäfer, and what I'd subsequently found in Schäfer's office. Joy let me talk without interruption, knowing I much preferred it that way.

"OK, I think I know where you're going here," she said. "It's really easy to imagine a narrative where Ali is a spy, spiriting out reports to be copied and passed on, and that Schäfer is her handler."

"Yes, it is," I said unhappily. "She has means and opportunity, but I don't see what motive she has. The very opposite, in fact."

"Assuming her backstory is true," Joy pointed out.

"Fair point. I'm waiting to hear back from Morgan on that," I told her. "I should have asked him to check on her story about her brother serving with the RAF, too. Could you pass that request on to him?"

"Sure, but that could take weeks to come back."

"I know, I'm just trying to turn over every stone. I have no doubt Schäfer is up to something questionable, but I need something more than an unusual locked case before I start throwing out accusations. Especially as I can't think of a motive for a German to help the Soviets. It seems like there is a great deal of mutual hostility between them."

"It could be as simple as money," said Joy.

"I suppose so. I guess some people's loyalties are easily negotiable."

"But here's another narrative for you. I'm with you on Schäfer, but assume Ali is on the level. She finds out something suspicious about him, and now he's threatening her to make her keep quiet."

"That could work, I think. I do want to be careful not to dismiss the other version though, just because this one allows me to feel better about Ali."

"Here's another thought to chew on. Maybe Ali shared whatever she knows with Caroline, and the attack on her was a warning to keep quiet. Maybe it accidentally went too far."

"Yes, that works," I said. "Or the other way around, Caroline found something out and told Ali. And Schäfer can't risk drawing attention with another attack, so now he is limited to intimidation and threats. And maybe the threatening Valentine's card suggests somebody thinks I know too. After all, I shared a room with Caroline and I'm with Ali much of the time."

"Yeah, that works too."

"There's one more thing that bothers me. When I asked Ali what she and Schäfer were arguing about, she fobbed me off with a story about him not liking her work, which makes no sense. She doesn't type up the reports, she just files them. It's a terrible lie, but given the circumstances, maybe it was the best she could come up with in that moment?"

"Or maybe it was deliberately bad, and she's asking for your help?" said Joy.

"That's a coded message that's a bit too subtle for me," I replied, "but you might be on to something."

I promised to call Joy again in a couple of days, even if I had nothing new, and we said our goodbyes.

I knew I should also update Morgan about Schäfer, but I decided that could wait until Monday. There was no reason to interrupt his weekend. Neither Schäfer nor I were going anywhere. I went back to the dorm and whiled away the day reading, chatting with the other girls, and worrying about everything I'd learned in my first week here. I was hoping that my brain might quietly work on it all in the background, and fit some puzzle pieces into place.

By the time dinner came around, I was no wiser than before. I changed into my party dress and met up with Ali for a drink and then dinner. She was wearing a classic little black dress, a simple knee length sheath that was sleeveless with a high, round neckline. It went perfectly with the shoes I had lent her and she thanked me again for helping her out. She was wearing minimal makeup, just enough to accentuate her pale skin and fine cheekbones. She looked beautiful, and I told her so. She blushed.

I was wearing a pair of scarlet flats—definitely not ruby, and the first person to make a *Wizard of Oz* joke was going to hear the sharp end of my temper. I hoped they worked okay with my dress, which was also black, below the knee with a slightly flared skirt. It was a favorite for dancing. I was better at appreciating clothes than picking them out for myself, and I wished that Ginnie had been there to advise me.

I had my inevitable social anxiety about the party, not least the fact that there would be many people there whose names I was expected to know but still did not remember. It was giving me a lump in my stomach, a pain behind the eyes, and an urge to run away. I told myself it would be no worse than the dances I had been to at college, and perhaps I could get Ali to whisper in my ear if I really needed to know a name. It didn't help much; I wasn't able to get much dinner inside me. What little I did, I hoped I could keep down.

We walked over to the party together. The club had been mostly emptied of its usual tables and chairs, the remainder pushed out to the edges of the room to clear a space for dancing. The staff had dressed up the tables with candles and small glasses with a couple of flowers in each. I supposed that was what passed for romantic on an army base. And from somewhere, they had located red, white, and blue bunting, possibly left over from VE and VJ Day celebrations, and had hung it around the room. The effect was more 4th of July than 14th of February, but at least they had made an effort. The band was tuning up, and small groups of people were standing around the floor, drinking and gossiping, or sitting at tables doing the same. The sound of chatter was already distressingly loud. If the small dance floor was too busy, even the dancing might not be much fun, I thought ruefully.

I needed a drink. With Ali trailing behind, I made my way over to the bar, trying as much as possible not to brush against other people, nodding and mouthing "Hello" at the ones I knew to speak to.

"Rye, straight, the good stuff," I told the barman. The barman was new, not in uniform, and possibly a professional brought in for the evening. He gave me a sideways look that I didn't like at all.

"Are you sure, miss?" he asked. "Wouldn't you prefer a cocktail?"

I took a beat to avoid saying anything he'd regret now and I'd regret later. My tolerance for men suggesting that my choice of drink was inappropriate was absolutely zero at the best of times, and this was not the best of times.

"Make it a double," I said. Judging by the way the room was filling up, I was going to need it. He shrugged and poured. "And a vodka for my friend," I added.

Ali and I found a bit of clear floorspace away from the bar and stood quietly, watching the room fill up. The women were in their party frocks and the men in suits or uniforms. It wasn't Ginnie's New Year's party by any stretch, but people were doing their best and most of them seemed to be enjoying themselves. I wished I knew how they did it. Ali seemed as reluctant as me to mingle. From time to time, some of the other girls would come over and chat with us for a while. Fran and Liz talked dresses and dances and dates, and I was relieved to have remembered their names. Some of the girls from Caroline's clique stopped by and I smiled my way through essentially the same conversation again. Nothing was too demanding so far, but every interaction drained my emotional glass a little. Ali stepped away to fetch herself another vodka, and Lewis stepped in.

"Hello, Dot," he said. "I haven't seen much of you since we chatted over dinner."

I nodded and smiled. I wasn't sure how—or even if—I was supposed to respond to that, although the silence that followed suggested that I should have filled it with something.

"Anyway," continued Lewis, once the silence was long enough to be awkward, "I was thinking it would be nice to go into town next week. I can usually get a car."

"That must be handy," I replied, slipping again into my bookstore voice. Joy had told me it was perfectly polite and pleasant, while firmly indicating that nothing more than a professional relationship was going on. That was exactly what I wanted right now. Another silence followed while my brain worked furiously to try to decode this conversation. Was Lewis trying to ask me for a date? Or was he just telling me he liked driving into town? Would that be a normal thing for somebody to like? If a date was what he was trying to insinuate, I wished he would just ask directly so that I could say "No" and move on with my evening. How was this code so effortless for other people?

My train of thought was derailed by the return of Ali, a fresh drink in hand, and the realization that a young man in an ill-fitting suit was approaching us. I anticipated a request for one of us to dance with him. He was a couple of inches taller than me, slim, and dark haired. There was something vaguely Slavic and not unhandsome about his looks.

"Good evening, Miss Babinski," he said, his German accent immediately obvious.

Ali nodded, but did not otherwise return his greeting. I realized that his suit had probably been provided to him by the army. Many of the Germans here had been evacuated at short notice and allowed to bring very few of their own possessions with them.

He turned to me. "Miss Stone, my name is Rolf Weber. Will you perhaps dance with me?"

My reluctance must have been written all over my face.

"Please," he continued, "our countries are no longer enemies. It is time for reconciliation, no?"

In as level a voice as I could manage, I replied, "That depends very much on what you did during the war."

"So, yes, I understand. There are certainly men here who have done crimes, or even brutalities, that are overlooked because of their usefulness to America. If you will, I shall tell you my history while we dance, and then you can judge for yourself whether I am one of them."

His request was reasonable. And it was also a chance to gather more intel about the Germans, perhaps even Schäfer. I swallowed my distaste and offered him my hand, and he led me out onto the dance floor. It took him a few moments to find the beat, partly because the band was having trouble finding it too, and then he jumped in. His dancing was competent and unremarkable, and left me free to concentrate on his story.

"I was a college student when the war began. I graduated with a degree in mechanical engineering in 1942, and was immediately drafted into the army. Germany did not much value scientists or engineers at that time, and many people, even with higher degrees, were sent to the infantry. Because I was an engineer, I was assigned to drive a truck, naturally. Drivers were expected to be their own mechanics in the field, as the army thought that this was what engineers did. In the winter of that year, my regiment was sent to the eastern front. From the time we arrived, it was an almost constant retreat. Every week came news of more losses. Many of us believed that before long, we would be defending Berlin itself. Of course, to say such things out loud was to ask for a firing squad."

"That must have been dispiriting," I offered, mostly to let him know I was still listening. "But what does that have to do with Paperclip?"

"So then in 1943, Hitler decided that he needed new weapons. He was obsessed with *Wunderwaffe*—wonder weapons that would change the war in one stroke. He wanted massive tanks, bigger missiles, rocket planes, all kinds of technological miracles. Suddenly scientists and engineers were valuable again, and they recalled us from the front. But the whole effort was chaos. Nobody seemed to be in charge. Many weapons were started, but never finished. Some were completely ridiculous from the beginning. There was huge waste of resources that could have gone to real weapons, but we did not care about that. We only cared that we had the chance to escape the fighting. The rocket people were the most valuable for Hitler, but the rest of us were also assigned to projects."

"What did you get assigned to?"

"Hitler wanted jet fighters that could stop the Allies' bombers. I was assigned to that. Again, there was no control. There were too many designs and too few prototypes, and it was obvious Germany did not have the material or factories to make many such planes, even if the designs succeeded. Nothing I worked on ever flew. But anyway, I learned a lot about jet engines, so here I am. Many people here can tell you stories like mine."

"I heard a story that all the scientists wanted to surrender to the Americans. Is that true?" Morgan had told me his version of that, but I wanted to hear it directly from the German side.

"Who else would we surrender to? We despised the French, we were terrified of the Soviets, and the British could not afford us. That left the Americans." I got the impression from how readily he rolled this out that it was sort of a standard joke among the Germans.

I had to admit that, if Rolf's story were true, he was guilty of nothing more than avoiding fighting on the front lines of Hitler's war, and I couldn't really blame anybody for that. I guess he read something on my face, because he spoke again. "Please do not think we are all monsters. Only some of us."

The tune came to an end, and everybody politely clapped for the band. I realized that we had ended up not far from a table where Schäfer and three other Germans were sitting, and Schäfer looked angry again. He beckoned Rolf over and I trailed along behind. Immediately, he began to berate him loudly in German while the others looked on sternly. German is an excellent language for angry words.

"Weber! I have told you before, you are not to fraternize with the American women!"

"Schäfer," he replied, smiling calmly, *"I have told you before that I do not take instructions from you."*

Schäfer became even redder at this breach of German manners. *"You will address me as Herr Doktor. Or if you prefer, you may call me Major,"* he shouted.

Rolf was openly smirking now. *"We are no longer in the army, Schäfer. Or in your case, perhaps the SS?"*

Before Schäfer could protest further, Rolf turned to me. "Thank you for the dance. In return, may I buy you a drink?"

I nodded, and he led the way through the crowd towards the bar. I followed in his wake. As we approached, the background chatter was interrupted by shouting, in English this time. A small crowd had gathered to watch the spectacle. Rolf pushed through the crowd and I slipstreamed behind him. Standing at the bar was the tall, thin figure of Bill. He had a nearly-full glass of beer in one hand which sloshed and splashed as he gesticulated.

"And let me tell you another thing!" he said, shaking his glass in the face of a bemused bystander. He was very obviously drunk.

"Let me tell you!" he repeated. "Those criminals get all the glory. All the respect. Eckert, Vogt, Amtmann. The brass just love them. Give them everything they want. Hard-working Americans? Pffft." With that last, he sprayed the closest spectators with some mixture of saliva and beer.

"And you know what else? They are paid more than us! Do you know what they are paying us? Do you?" he demanded of the bemused onlookers.

He was about to launch into another tirade—or possibly repeat the same one over—when Lewis slipped out of the crowd and sidled up beside him. He placed a hand on his upper arm.

"Come on now, Bill. Calm down," he said. "Let's all enjoy the party."

"You let go of me!" Bill shouted, wrenching his arm free and spilling more beer in the process. "It's all your fault!"

"Bill, this isn't helping," said Lewis, calmly.

Bill shoved Lewis away with his free hand, then tried to punch him. It was a looping, ungainly swing that took a long time to come around. Lewis stepped out of its range easily and, as Bill attempted to untangle his own arms, stepped in, picked his spot, and landed a fast jab on Bill's jaw. Bill went straight down, his legs folding under him like a collapsing deckchair. His glass hit the floor, shattering and scattering shards of glass and splashes of beer in every direction.

The crowd was silent. People began to drift away, in search of fresh amusement.

"Could somebody help me put Bill to bed?" Lewis asked. A couple of men in civvies stepped forward. "And somebody get a mop and clean this mess up."

Rolf bought me the drink he had promised, I thanked him, and made my way back to Ali.

"What do you make of all that?" I asked her.

Ali just shrugged. "It is not the first time. Bill drinks much, but he does not drink well. I think it gets worse each time."

An alcoholic with a grievance sounded like a red flag for a security risk to me. I also recalled what Lewis had told me over dinner, that Bill was off on a project of his own that nobody else much cared about. So why keep him around? I would love to get a look at his file.

I was briefly tempted to slip away right then and pay another illicit visit to my office, but it was too much of a risk. If Bill's folder was in with the general files, rather than the black cabinet, I would surely have a chance to peek at it on Monday. I also reminded myself to call Morgan on Monday to bring him up to date. Then I set my mind to trying to enjoy the remainder of the party as best I could.

Chapter Ten

I called Morgan promptly on Monday morning, at eight for me and five for him. I was impressed that he was again there to call me back. I had been taught that 'on time' was late, and 'five minutes early' was on time. Apparently, he'd graduated from the same school.

"I have something for you on Lewis, and it's a bit disturbing to me. It turns out he was flagged by the FBI a couple of years ago for his continuing association with known communists," Morgan told me.

"And did OSS know? Why is he still there?"

"I don't know. I can't find any trace of the report here. I only know about it because I had asked the FBI directly about him and they telexed me a copy."

I pondered that for a few seconds, and did not like the implications I was drawing.

"I have something for you too," I said. I told him about the incident in the bar between Ted and Bill. "What could Bill mean by blaming Lewis?"

"I have no idea, but it doesn't look good. I'll see what else I can find on Doctor Reardon. Give me a couple of days."

"Okay, thank you. And I'll see if I can sneak a peek at his personnel file here. By the way, did you get anything back on Ali Babinski?"

"Not much, I'm afraid. The part of her story about how she was admitted to the US bears up, but I can't go any further back than that without a much larger investigation. The staffing on this one is just you, me, and your friend Joy."

"Maybe you can also look into one of the scientists here for me, a Doctor Schäfer. Sorry, no first name. Schäfer is a pretty common German name, so if there is more than one, I'm looking at the one in aerodynamics."

We ended the conversation and I sat pensively in the phone booth for a while. There were too many possible scenarios, and while several people here looked bad to me, I had nothing concrete on anybody. I needed to figure out a way to advance at least one of these lines of investigation. All I could do right now, though, was have a coffee and a Kool before getting to work.

The rest of Monday passed routinely. I managed to get a look at Bill's file when Ali stepped outside for a cigarette—Mrs. Worthington had forbidden smoking inside—but found nothing extraordinary. His periodic security evaluations were bland, with no mention of his drinking, and his research contributions rated as unexceptional. I slogged through my day, had my usual drink with Ali, and then sat with some of the other girls at dinner where the conversation circled around who had danced with whom and what might develop from it. It was relentlessly trivial.

I needed a change of pace. I said my goodbyes and told them I going to the enlisted men's club for a drink. As coarse as the drivers' conversation could be, at least it wouldn't be about the damn dance. Ali looked at me plaintively, as if I were abandoning her to the gossip and chatter that bored her as much as it did me.

"Come with me, Ali," I said. "It'll be better if we're together."

She sat silently for several seconds, and just as I was giving up and turning away, she jumped up and joined me, putting her arm through mine. I was not exactly comfortable with that, but I didn't want to drive her off, so I tolerated it for the walk over to the club. Inside, it was quieter than the last time I'd been there. Half a dozen of the drivers from last time were at a table, including Ricky, whose name I remembered, to my surprise. He waved us over.

"Look who's back," he said with a broad smile, "and she's brought a friend."

"Hello Ricky," I said. "I'm sure you all remember Ali. If you're polite tonight, maybe we'll keep coming back." I hoped that didn't come across as schoolmarmish.

"Tommy, fetch the ladies some drinks," said Ricky. "Rye for Dot, and for Ali?" He looked up at her.

"Vodka," she said, her voice breaking. "Thank you," she added after a moment.

There was a rapid reshuffling of seats so that Ali and I could sit together in the middle of one bench, Ricky to my left and a place saved for Tommy to her right. The others, all of whom I recognized, and none of whose names I remembered, sat across from us.

"Sorry," I said, "as promised, I forgot everybody else's names."

Ali surprised me by jumping in, quickly rattling off the names. That seemed to impress the boys too, and as best I could tell, they warmed to her a little.

"We must have made a good impression last time," said one of them named Dan.

"Or a very bad one," said Ali, with a hint of a smile. I wasn't sure what was more surprising, her impressive memory for names, or seeing her so relaxed, especially after what she had said about her first encounter here. Perhaps having a supportive friend at her side made all the difference.

Tommy sat our drinks in front of us and rejoined us. "You ladies at the dance on Saturday?" he asked.

We both nodded.

"Did you see what happened with Bill Reardon?" he continued.

"He was badly drunk," said Ali.

"That's nothing new," said Dan from across the table.

"He was totally sauced," I said. "He was ranting about how the Germans get all the credit and nobody respects what the Americans are doing here. Ted Lewis tried to calm him down, and Bill took a swing at him."

"Did he connect?" asked Dan. He seemed quite enthusiastic about the prospect.

"He was so wild, he was lucky he didn't punch himself in the nose," I replied. That raised a small laugh. "After that, Ted knocked him out. One punch." That seemed to impress a few of them.

"Okay," I went on, "do we get a story in return?"

"I've got one I think you'll like," said the man on Dan's left. "It's about Hathaway."

"The dumbest man in Intelligence," said somebody at the end of the table to general agreement.

"Anyway," continued the storyteller, "I had to drive him into town last week."

"He could not drive himself?" asked Ali.

"No, and here's why. He's been taking a car every Wednesday night for months now, and a couple of weeks ago, he brought it back with a big dent in the fender. That's the second time, so the base commander told us he couldn't sign a car out any longer. He had to have a driver."

"Was he drunk?" I asked.

"No, I think he's just a lousy driver." That got a big laugh.

Or maybe he was a hit-and-run driver, my brain was screaming at me. I desperately wanted to ask whether this happened the night Barbara was hit, and what color his car was, but I couldn't see any way to do that without it sounding really weird and scaring up a flock of suspicions.

"Anyway, last Wednesday I get detailed to drive him. We go into town and he has me drop him in front of a seedy-looking joint, tells me to pick him up in two hours. Naturally, I'm wondering what a nice captain like him is doing in a place like that, so as soon as the door closes behind him, I scoot out of the car and press my nose up against the window of the place. I see him go straight past the bar and through a door in the back.

"Okay, so now I'm really curious. I wait five minutes to see if comes back out, but he no-shows. So much for that, I figure. I go to the pool hall, shoot a game, have a beer, and come back for him at the end of the night. So what do you guys think is going on in the back?"

"Was this place on 4th, near Brown?" asked Ricky.

"Yeah, how'd you guess?"

"There's a backroom poker game there most nights. High stakes, way too rich for a working stiff like me."

"They must love him there," said Dan.

Everybody but Ali and I seemed to get the joke.

Dan must have noticed our confusion. "Hathaway is a terrible poker player. Some of the officers have a game on base—just playing for pennies, and the loser brings a bottle of whiskey to the next game. And it's almost always him bringing the bottle to the next game."

"How can he afford it?"

"Beats me. He's definitely not from money."

If Hathaway was losing a lot of money playing poker badly, could that mean he had money problems? Might he be borrowing money from the wrong people? That seemed like a thread I wanted to tug on if I could figure out how. Frankly, this whole base felt like it had more red flags than a Moscow parade.

Ali and I stayed another couple of hours, and the drivers were mostly well-behaved. I went to bed with one more mystery and no more answers.

Tuesday morning started well. Ali seemed more cheerful than I had seen her in days. Perhaps she was putting the argument with Schäfer behind her. Or perhaps she had enjoyed the company last night more than she had expected. Either way, I was happy to see her smile.

Around three in the afternoon, we were interrupted by the same orderly I'd met twice before. Once again, he spoke briefly with Mrs. Worthington, then asked me to come with him. We headed for Hathaway's office. I was beginning to suspect that the orderly had a fulltime job running errands for him.

I sat down and we exchanged pleasantries. The captain looked a lot more relaxed than the last time I had seen him.

"Miss Stone, I will make this brief," he said. "We have identified the source of the leaks from this base and will be taking care of the matter quietly. Mr. Morgan would like you to call him this evening for instructions, but I imagine you will be free to leave. You are to behave as if nothing unusual has happened for as long as you remain here. I'm sure I don't need to remind you that you are still sworn to secrecy over this whole affair. It would be bad for morale if word got around that there had ever been a leak here."

I looked at him for several long seconds. *Bad for your reputation you mean*, I thought. Everything about his statement seemed very unlikely. Perhaps I was being an intellectual snob, but I found it hard to credit that Hathaway had caught a spy under my nose.

"I assume you're not at liberty to tell me who the spy is nor how you found him out," I said eventually.

"You are correct," he replied. He seemed to be enjoying that part.

"Can I at least say goodbye to my friends here?"

"I suppose so, provided you say nothing about this whole business, especially your own role."

"What should I tell people if they ask why I'm leaving so soon after arriving?"

"I don't know, make up something about a family emergency," he said, waving his hand dismissively. "Anyway, that's all."

I nodded, stood up, and left. It was a thoroughly unsatisfactory situation, but there didn't appear to be anything I could do about it. Not only had my research into the leak been useless, but any chance of solving the death of Barbara or the attack on Caroline was out the window. Perhaps I would learn more from Morgan later. In the meantime, I had a head full of loose threads.

I spent the remainder of the day impatiently filing personnel records and chasing thoughts around my head. I could have slacked off, but it wasn't in my nature to leave a mess behind for whoever my successor was. When five o'clock finally came around, Ali and I went through our lockup ritual. I asked her to wait for me for a moment as I had to take care of something before I could leave. I knocked on Mrs. Worthington's door and waited several moments before she summoned me in.

I stood in front of her desk; it did not seem like a good idea to presume I could sit down without express permission.

"Mrs. Worthington, I'm afraid I have some bad news," I began. "I have a family emergency and have to go home immediately. I'm sorry about letting you down like this."

I handed her my keys.

"I shall be sorry to see you go," she replied. "You have been very efficient while you've been here, and the backlog is almost entirely gone. I shan't ask what your emergency is. I just hope we have better luck holding on to your replacement."

"Thank you," I said. I felt a little pulse of pride at this rare praise from Mrs. Worthington. I pushed away a mental picture of myself backing out of her presence, bowing.

"What was that about?" Ali asked me when I emerged.

"I'll tell you over a drink," I said. I needed a drink first, and then I would call Morgan.

Once we were set up at the bar and had our cigarettes lit, Ali asked me again.

"Sorry to do this to you," I said, "but I have to leave the base."

She looked distressed enough that even I could tell. Perhaps she was even close to tears. I suspected that I might be the only true friend she had here as much as she was mine.

"How soon?" she asked.

"Right away. Maybe tomorrow, maybe Thursday."

"What is the reason?"

"It's a family emergency," I said. I was going to leave it at that, but then I added, "My mother is in the hospital."

"Your mother?" she replied. "But I thought—" She met my eyes for a moment, and stopped. "Oh. I understand. I too worry about my parents. Very much."

I hoped she had decoded my message.

"Anyway, if you ever find yourself in Los Angeles, look me up. I need to make a call about my travel arrangements now."

I settled myself into a phone booth and called Morgan for what was probably the last time.

"Sorry about this," he said, "but I have to pull you out. Case closed."

"This makes no sense," I replied. "There are so many loose ends here. I have to tell you—"

"Not right now," he interrupted. "We'll debrief in person when you're back. My office on Monday at nine, okay?"

Morgan had to have some good reason for not wanting to talk details over the phone, so I didn't fight it.

"Very well. I'll deliver my final report then."

"Thank you. There will be a ticket for you at the airport tomorrow morning. Please feel free to take a cab to the airport and put it on your expense report."

"Thanks," I said, "but I'm pretty sure I can get a ride."

I rejoined Ali and finished my drink pensively. We went to dinner together and sat by ourselves. I tried to think of who else on the base I wanted to say goodbye to. The list was very short. When we were done, I asked her to come to the enlisted men's club with me again.

After I shared the news with Ricky, Tommy, Dan, and the others, there was some good-natured banter over who would take me to the airport, with Tommy finally winning out. Even though I'd only spent two evenings with them, I felt like I would miss them, even the ones whose names I had not managed to memorize. They bought drinks all night for Ali and me, and by the end of the evening, I knew I was going to have a hangover in the morning. As we got up to leave, I tugged on Ricky's sleeve and drew him aside.

"Please be kind to Ali," I said. "She's starting to like you guys, and she doesn't have a lot of other friends here."

"No problem," said Ricky. "Hey, is it true about the homicide detective?" he asked.

"Very much so," I replied. Despite everything else, I was looking forward to seeing Eddie again, not to mention Joy and Ginnie.

Chapter Eleven

I arrived at the Lockheed Air Terminal on Thursday in the early afternoon. LA sunlight was streaming through the windows, and darkening clouds were banked up over the hills. It looked like the afternoon showers were going to start their routine right on cue. I was happy to be back in a climate where my raincoat would be adequate protection against the elements, but unhappy about everything else connected to the end of this truncated investigation. Perhaps my forthcoming debrief with Morgan would put my questions to rest, but knowing the intelligence community's obsession with compartmentalization, I very much doubted it. They would feel no obligation to explain themselves to me.

As I lugged my suitcase through the arrivals hall, I saw a clutch of anonymous men in dark suits and chauffeurs' caps holding up signs with names written on them in large black letters. Limo drivers waiting for their pickups. To my surprise, one of them read 'STONE.' Had Morgan generously arranged a car for me, perhaps as a 'thank you' for the work I'd done, even though I hadn't delivered the result he'd requested?

Right then, I heard a familiar voice calling out my name. To my delight, it was Joy. She was wearing her usual outfit, but on her head was her cab driver's cap, something I hadn't seen since she quit driving for a living to join me at the agency. I put down my bag and allowed her to give me a hug. She knew me well enough not to hold onto it for too long.

"Good to see you, kid," she said.

"You too," I replied. "What are you doing here?"

"I told Madge you were coming back from a long trip, and she let me borrow a cab to pick you up."

Madge was the dispatcher at Red Star, the cab company where Joy used to drive when I first met her.

"What's with the cap?" I asked.

"It's so some overeager cop won't pull me over, thinking I stole the cab."

I wasn't sure if that was a joke, so I just let it go.

"Come on," continued Joy. "The car's right outside and I don't want to get a ticket. Also, the meter's running." That last part was definitely a joke. She insisted on taking the suitcase from me, and I didn't fight too hard.

We were fifteen minutes from the airport when I realized I hadn't told the limo driver I didn't need him. *Never mind*, I told myself. *I'm sure it will sort itself out.*

We dropped my bag at my apartment, then returned the car to the Red Star Taxi garage. I took a moment to thank Madge and promised to catch up with her properly soon. I told Joy I was too tired to get any office work done, and she offered to join me in a drink and a cigarette while I caught her up on the case and its abrupt termination. Inside Jack's, we scrambled awkwardly up onto a couple of barstools at a hightop. Getting up there was never elegant, but once perched, I liked the feeling of being up high. I got a Kool going and took a slug of my rye. Joy lit up a Lucky Strike.

"Thanks again for being my lifeline on this case," I said. "I'm sorry to put you through all the probing of your social life. I should have thought about that before I pushed Morgan to read you in. And all that to just have it end like this." Even though she had told me she was a lesbian months ago, Joy remained very private about her dating life, and I didn't press her on it. At this point Morgan probably knew more about who she was seeing than I did.

"Hey, no problem," she replied, and took a mouthful of beer.

"How was Morgan about it? Did he not find out? Or just not care? I don't even know if the intelligence services have a policy on homosexuality."

Joy shrugged. "He told me it wasn't an issue. As long as he knew, and I knew that he knew, there was no possibility of somebody holding it over me."

"Can I ask you one question, though? How did you get into the WASP? We both know how the military is about it."

"Funny thing. We were technically civilians. They didn't even ask."

"What?" I said, stunned. "So you don't get veteran status? Or benefits?"

"Nope. We were treated like military in pretty much every way while we served, and some of us even have service ribbons to show for it. But the moment they decided they didn't need us any more, they 'remembered' we were just civilians."

"That seems really unfair."

"It is. Hey, I get to ask you a personal question in return. Something that's been in the back of my mind for a long time."

"Okay. You can ask, but I can't promise I'll answer."

"I know how much you don't like being touched. But how do you deal with it when you're dancing?"

"Oh. That's… different. With a dance partner, I know where the hands are supposed to go, and how long they are supposed to stay there. If a guy's hands stray, I let him know about it right away. And there's no emotional or romantic subtext that I have to decode, like, say, when a guy tries to put his hand on my shoulder."

"I think I get it. It's like it's scripted, so it's safe. What about when a guy wants to dance close?"

"Like, bodies touching?" I shivered at the thought. "That completely freaks me out. I push away, hard. And if the guy resists, he gets my heel on his toe. Although I make an exception for Eddie." That reminded me, I really wanted to call Eddie before the night was over and let him know I was back.

"Good for you," smiled Joy. "It's great to see the two of you together."

"Okay, now we need to talk a little about the case," I said, pulling my notebook from my purse. As always, I had a low tolerance for the social prologues that most people seemed to enjoy when there was work to be done. "I need to write up a final report for Morgan, and it would help me a lot to get my thoughts straight if we can walk through it together." It was mid-afternoon and we had the place to ourselves, so I wasn't worried about being overheard.

"Sure. But let's get fresh drinks before we start."

Joy was gone only a minute before she returned with a rye for me and another beer for herself.

"Okay. Lay it out for me," she said.

"Let's start with the easy one. Schäfer definitely has something funny going on, with his weird case locked away in his office."

"Yeah, but that's not nearly enough to accuse him of treason. Wait, is it treason if a German sells American secrets to the Soviets?"

"I think the word is treachery," I replied. "Anyway, you're right. But I couldn't get into his case without it being obvious I'd tampered with the padlock. I'll put it in the report, and maybe that'll be enough for Morgan to reopen the case. Then he can call Schäfer in to answer some questions. But the risk is, if he does that and Schäfer is not our guy, the real spy goes to ground for who knows how long."

"Now how does Ali fit in? It's easy to see how she could be providing material to Schäfer, who then copies it and gets it out… somehow, we still have to figure that out."

"Or she could be, like we said earlier, just somebody who knows about Schäfer. Maybe he's threatening her to keep her quiet."

"That would mean he's getting material some other way. Maybe Ali caught him stealing from her files? Either way, the bad lie she told you still makes me think she wants to get caught. It's a way to ask for help without making it obvious to Schäfer."

"She definitely seems like an unwilling participant, whatever her role," I replied. I paused for a sip of rye and a pull on my cigarette. "But what could Schäfer be holding over her? If it were just physical threats, she could go straight to the MPs with a complaint. I wish I'd had a chance to have that conversation with Ali. But I couldn't see a way to do it without exposing myself, which would be disastrous if we're wrong about her."

"It smells really bad, but it doesn't add up to a whole lot. Who else do we have?"

"I can't dismiss Mrs. Worthington. She's first in the office in the morning, last to leave at night, and holds all the keys, including the only one to the confidential black cabinet. I'll bet she knows where everybody's skeletons are buried, if she needs leverage. I really wonder what she's up to all day behind that closed office door."

"Yeah," said Joy, "if you'd had more time, a look around her office could have been very useful. What else?"

"We have Lewis with his communist connections, and Bill with his anger and drinking problems. Maybe Lewis is protecting Bill and in return, Bill is providing him with reports."

"Bill seems like a poor choice for a source," Joy pointed out. "He sounds like a sloppy drunk, and that makes him unreliable. Unless Bill is the best Lewis can get. I don't think many people would risk treason just for a little protection for their bad habits."

"Perhaps Bill's getting more than that out of it. You mentioned before about people betraying secrets for the attention, and Bill definitely feels under-respected by his American bosses as well as ostracized by the Germans."

"You think maybe Lewis has sold him a line about the Soviets appreciating his genius? And Lewis is directing Bill to mix in other reports too so it's not obvious that he's the source. In fact, I'll bet the Soviets don't give a bean for

Bill's work, and it's just a sop to get him to work for them. It's the other stuff they really want. Is Hathaway in on it with them?"

"Maybe. At first, I thought that Lewis would be under Hathaway's thumb because of his communist history. But perhaps it's the other way around. After all, Lewis just plays dumb. But Hathaway really is dumb. If Hathaway has money problems from a gambling itch he needs to scratch, and Bill is the one bankrolling him, that might buy a lot of cooperation."

"A man could get away with an awful lot with the head of security covering for him," said Joy.

"Damn, I wish I knew how Hathaway dented those cars," I replied. "If he was the one that killed Barbara, he's perfectly placed to bury the investigation. But if Hathaway isn't working with Lewis, it might really have been a simple accident after all. If only I could lock Hathaway in an interrogation room with Eddie for fifteen minutes."

"What else?" she asked.

"There's the attack on Caroline, which seems like a weird outlier."

"Yeah. It feels like it's a piece from a different puzzle entirely."

"Maybe it is. One thing we've learned in this business is that not everything means something. I don't like the fact that it happened almost as soon as I started investigating, but sometimes coincidences do happen, however much I dislike them."

"What now?"

"My brain is itching in so many places I can't scratch right now, but my stomach is telling me I need to get some dinner before I have anything more to drink. Also, I need to call Eddie and see if he's free on Saturday. And then let's come back here and spend the night with Madge and the boys. It's going to feel good to be among friends, and not to worry whether I'm being watched."

Chapter Twelve

By the time Monday rolled around, I was beginning to feel like my life was returning to its regular rhythms. I was sleeping in my own bed, showering in private, and eating decent food on my own schedule. Eddie had taken me out for dinner and then dancing on Saturday, which had been absolutely lovely. It was frustrating not to be able to pick his brains about the case, but at least he understood the constraints of working undercover, and didn't press me about it. Joy and I fueled up on coffee and cigarettes before catching a streetcar over to the Federal building.

Morgan met us in the lobby of the former OSS office and showed us into a small conference room. There was a worn table with a thin veneer over its cheap wood decorated with coffee rings and half a dozen chairs set around it. Probably yet another war issue piece, and overdue for replacement. We seated ourselves.

"Coffee?" asked Morgan. "I don't recommend it, to be honest."

I'd had enough government issue coffee for one lifetime, and I was happy to decline. Joy did the same. I handed him my report.

"Here's what I have, such as it is. Nothing conclusive, but a couple of leads I feel like somebody should pursue."

He didn't open it. He put it in a manila folder that he pushed to one side.

"I promised you a debrief, but it's going to be frustratingly little, I'm afraid," he said. "Hathaway got a tip-off, and found classified documents concealed in somebody's dorm room. He notified me, and my director ordered me to pull you out and shut down the operation."

"You know that makes no sense, right?"

"Rest assured, I'm as frustrated as you are. But I'm sorry, I really can't talk about it any further." And then he silently mouthed, *not here.*

I exchanged a glance with Joy to see if she had caught that too.

"If we're not going to see you again, at least let us buy you a decent cup of coffee and say goodbye properly," said Joy. Their eyes met and some sort of communication took place that I missed out on entirely. This was one of the many moments I was grateful to have Joy by my side.

"That would be okay," he replied, "as long as we don't talk about anything confidential. Understood?"

"Perfectly," said Joy.

He took my report to Wardour's secretary, and returned with his fedora on his head and his trench coat slung over one arm. We walked in silence the few blocks to Café del Sol, a small coffee shop that Eddie had introduced us to last year. We'd been back many times since. We stepped inside and Mrs. Mendez, the owner, smiled and greeted us cheerfully. She was short, stout, very brown, with hair so black it sucked up sunlight.

"The usual for you two, yes? And what would your friend like?"

"Yes, please. And he's going to try the same," I replied. Morgan raised his eyebrows, but didn't object. Our 'usual' was café de olla, a dark, sweet brew spiced with cinnamon, cloves, and star anise, served in a beautiful clay pot. The only downside was that after drinking it, you would regret every other cup of coffee you had in your life, before or since.

"Okay, Mr. Morgan, something's going on," I said. "You didn't want to talk on the phone, and you didn't want to talk at your office. And now we're in a coffee shop where you don't want to talk about anything confidential."

Joy and Morgan exchanged smiles.

"What?" I asked, my forehead creased in bafflement.

"I told you," Joy said to Morgan, "she doesn't pick up on that kind of subtlety."

"Oh," I said, as the realization clicked into place. "We are here to talk about something confidential."

"I have to be very clear, what I'm doing now is breaking several rules, so we are very much off the record," said Morgan. "I'm off the case, no further investigation, and I certainly shouldn't be talking to you two about it. And as long as we're off the record, you can call me Daniel."

"And you can call us Dot and Joy."

At that moment, Mrs. Mendez arrived with our coffees. Daniel looked at his dubiously, and took a sniff.

"That's... very different."

"Trust us on this," said Joy. "You're going to like it."

Daniel took a sip, a pause, and then a bigger mouthful.

"Great," he said sardonically. "I discover this place just in time to be relocated to D.C."

My patience for preliminaries expired.

"So what happened at the TDL?" I asked.

"Like I said at the office, Captain Hathaway received a tip about someone from a so-called reliable informant. He declined to name his source for what he described as 'operational reasons,' which I read as him wanting to keep all the credit. When they went to search the man's room, they found him dead, and several confidential papers concealed behind a drawer in the dresser."

"Who was the dead man?" I asked.

"A young engineer named Rolf Weber."

Suddenly I had a heavy lump in my stomach. I barely knew him, but the news shook me. From just our one dance, he seemed like such a gentle and thoughtful man.

"How did he die?" asked Joy.

"It looks like he overdosed, probably a combination of alcohol and sleeping pills," said Daniel. "We won't know for sure until we get the medical examiner's report."

I looked over at Joy. That story was disturbingly reminiscent of a case we dealt with last year that was very personal to her. Her father had been murdered with an overdose of barbiturates, and then the scene had been set up to look like he hanged himself. Was this bringing back bad memories for her? Nothing showed on her face, or at least nothing I could interpret.

"Shouldn't Hathaway have waited for instructions from you?" said Joy.

"Absolutely. Normally, if we found one spy, we'd leave him alone and observe so we could figure out who he was working with. But that was all blown up once word of Weber's death got around. Anybody else involved will inevitably shut down until they feel it's safe to resume.

There's nothing for the bureau to do but close the case, and start over if the leaks appear again."

I felt even more dissatisfied with the story now than I had when Daniel had first told me I was off the case. I tried to fit the puzzle pieces together, but they simply didn't make any picture I could see.

Joy nudged me. "Hey, kid, your coffee's getting cold," she said.

I realized I'd been staring into space, something I do sometimes when my brain is solving problems for me. And apparently it had been going on long enough for Joy to want to bring me back to the table.

"Sorry about that," I said. "I was trying to think of a version of events where Rolf committing suicide makes sense, and I can't come up with one. I met Rolf. If he was a spy, I'm turning in my P.I. license."

"I don't believe it either. But is it possible that Weber was being forced to participate in something, and saw suicide as his only way out?" asked Daniel.

"I don't think so. First of all, Rolf had no respect for authority. He actively enjoyed tweaking the more senior Germans, even though it seemed risky. And he was ill-disciplined. As an asset, he'd be a liability. Nobody would be foolish enough to recruit him, willing or unwilling. But even if he were a spy, he couldn't possibly have been acting alone. He was pretty low level, so his legitimate access to material was very limited, and he had no way of getting anything out of the base."

"The latter is what I was thinking about," said Daniel.

"You have a theory?" Joy said to me.

"The only story that makes sense to me is that the real spy realized I was making enough progress to scare him. So he decided to frame somebody expendable, a relatively junior engineer, then arrange to have Hathaway find him with incriminating evidence. With the cat out of the bag, the bureau would then have to close the case and settle for finding one spy," I said.

"And conveniently, the suspect can't say anything in his defense," Joy added.

"Does that implicate Hathaway himself?" I mused out loud. "It's possible he deliberately made a lot of noise uncovering the documents in Rolf's room, knowing it would shut me down, rather than doing it quietly so I could continue investigating."

"That's a gloomy prospect," said Daniel.

"I have another version," said Joy. "Instead of some clever conspiracy, maybe Hathaway just goofed. Let's still assume Weber was framed, for the same reason Dot said. Whoever framed him comes to Hathaway with a tip, and he sees visions of glory and promotion floating before his eyes. So instead of contacting you for instructions, he goes off half-cocked and decides to pick up Weber himself. Dot, you said he didn't seem too bright."

"You could be right," said Daniel. "I don't know that it makes much difference, though. Either way, my director decides the operation is blown, since we have nobody to interrogate and no chance of picking up the rest of the ring, so he tells me to shut Dot down and pull her out."

"And either way, we still have a big open question," I said. "If Rolf didn't commit suicide, who killed him? It would be easy to point the finger at Schäfer. If he wanted a scapegoat, Weber would be an easy choice after the way he humiliated Schäfer. And from the sound of it, it wasn't the first time."

"True," said Joy, "but I also wouldn't rule out Lewis. Everything about him smells bad, especially his relationship with Reardon."

"Speaking of Lewis, that's another loose end. It seems that somebody inside the intelligence world is protecting him. You said yourself that somebody senior would have to had to vouch for him after his Communist Party associations. And that FBI report about him was buried by somebody in your bureau."

"That could be anybody in the bureau," said Daniel, the tension in his voice obvious. "Or even the FBI: who knows if they ever sent the report like they claim? Maybe they screwed up at their end, and now they're covering for their mistake. And besides, with all the chaos around OSS disbanding, the report could simply have been lost. A cockup is more likely than a conspiracy, in my mind."

Daniel seemed determined to push back on the suggestion of a traitor inside the bureau. I understood it a little, but I did wish that he would take a step back and examine the evidence objectively.

"Maybe it's nothing," I said, "but you know how I feel about coincidences."

Joy touched me on the shoulder. I had no idea why, and I shrugged her hand off.

"So what happens now?" asked Joy.

"I read Dot's report, write up my assessment, turn it in, and move on to whatever's next, I'm afraid. But I am going to commit my doubts to paper with my recommendation that the investigation continue. Wardour won't like it, but when it turns out that the TDL is still leaking, I don't want that blowing back on me."

"And the possible collaborator in the agency?" I asked.

Daniel's face was tense, possibly even angry. "I can't start an internal mole hunt on wild speculation. In any case, I wouldn't know who to take it to. If I take it up my reporting chain, I might be bringing my accusation directly to the traitor himself."

"Can you go to the FBI?" asked Joy.

"And say what to them? That a civilian associate thinks that maybe there might possibly be a spy in our agency, but all the evidence is circumstantial? If I bring the FBI in and I'm wrong, it will be the end of my career. And if I'm right, it will probably be the end of the bureau. A lot of people in Washington wanted us abolished entirely after the war, not transferred to State. This would give them the ammunition they need. If the bureau is going to survive this, it has to be done quietly. And one thing the FBI does not do is catch spies quietly."

He drained his coffee. "Listen, I have to get back to the office. For your own safety, don't do anything further on this case without talking to me, okay?"

He pulled out a business card and wrote his LA office number on the back. Then he stood up, gathered his hat and coat, and left.

Joy was looking at me with an expression that was definitely not happiness.

"I missed a signal, didn't I?" I said.

"When I touched you on the shoulder, that was supposed to tell you to drop the subject of an insider, because it was upsetting Daniel."

"I have no idea how I was supposed to decode that," I said. "But I'll try to remember it for next time."

There was a long silence before Joy spoke again. "You're not going to leave this alone, are you?" she said.

"Not if I can figure out any way to pursue it. Listen, this could—"

Joy interrupted me. "Stop. I know what you're going to say. You're going to tell me this could be dangerous, and that you'll understand if I want out of it. You should know by now there's no way I'm going to let you do this on your own. I'm with you all the way."

I stood up, came around the table, and gave her a hug. But only a brief one.

Chapter Thirteen

Some small part of my brain continued to worry away at the Paperclip case like a cat with a long-dead mouse that refuses to play any longer, but with no apparent way to investigate Rolf's death, I had to set that aside. I picked up some cases Joy had been working—the usual mix of cheating husbands, insurance frauds, office espionage, embezzlement, and dishonest domestic staff. There was even a guy who was sneaking around behind his wife's back because he was planning a surprise birthday party for her. The trickiest part of that one was letting her know she didn't have to worry without spoiling the surprise. Those sort of cases were all the bread-and-butter of our business, the kind of work that kept the rent paid and the bank account ticking over. Ginnie could easily afford to keep us going in perpetuity, but we all wanted the validation of knowing that our agency was a viable business and not an expensive hobby.

I would have killed for a really chewy blackmail plot.

That Wednesday, we met up with Ginnie for afternoon cocktails, which were routine for her but a rare treat for us. Ginnie had told us she wanted to get out of the Marmont—the hotel where she made her home these days—for a change of scene, so we took a Red Car over to the Polo Lounge at the Beverley Hills hotel. I was wearing my best dress; a dark blue number with a button-down bodice and pleated skirt. It was a hand-me-down from Ginnie, naturally. Joy looked uncomfortable in the deep blue cotton suit with a pencil skirt that I had insisted she buy for occasions where her regular outfit was inappropriate. This was one of those occasions. Although the Marmont was used to her turning up in her slacks and flight jacket, the Polo Lounge had a rigid dress code. Rumor had it that even Marlene Dietrich had been turned away when she showed up wearing pants.

Ginnie was there ahead of us. The perfectly coutured and coiffed hostess welcomed us with a measure of her professional warmth carefully calibrated to our appearance, and brought us over to Ginnie's table. We ordered drinks, a Manhattan for me and a bourbon on the rocks for Joy, and lit cigarettes.

"I expected the place to be ritzier," said Joy. "Where are all the glamorous socialites and celebrities?"

"It's out of season," replied Ginnie. "Most of the regular patrons are wintering in Palm Springs. As are most of my friends, actually. The New Year's Ball was a sort of unofficial end-of-season send-off."

"You didn't want to join them?"

"I really can't see myself sitting around the pool or being prodded in a spa for more than a couple of days, spending evenings with the same round of people I see here. Honestly, I'm beginning to think I don't actually like most my friends very much."

"Aren't you feeling a little bored here by yourself?"

"You have no idea. I've completely run out of movies. I've seen *The Blue Dahlia, Black Angel,* and every other shade of Noir you can name. I've seen *The Postman Always Rings Twice* three times, and if I watch *The Big Sleep* one more time, I might actually understand the plot."

"What about the symphony?" Joy asked. Ginnie was a major donor to the L.A. Philharmonic, and generally attended the opening night of every program.

"They're doing something incomprehensible by Stravinsky."

"No boyfriend right now?"

"I'm a bit off steady relationships since John, I think." John was John Dalton, a private eye whom Ginnie had been dating. His murder had been the catalyst that had brought Joy, Ginnie, and me together. I reflected that, remarkably, it had only been little over a year since those events, so it was understandable that Ginnie was not ready for a new relationship.

"Anyway," she continued, "the only attractive men around these days seem to be fortune hunters, gigolos, and penniless movie stars-in-waiting. I can get one of those whenever I want one. They might be good for the occasional date or for something pretty to dangle off my arm for an event, but sadly, they're not much use for anything else. Anyway, have you two been up to anything entertaining?"

I paused to consider how much I could tell her about my frustrating sojourn in Ohio. Would telling her nothing at all be kinder than teasing her with just a few details?

"I've been out of town on a project for the government, but unfortunately, I can't say much about it as it's classified," I said.

"Oh, that sounds intriguing," said Ginnie. "What can you share?"

"Gosh. Let's see. There were Nazis, Soviet spies, a murder, possibly two, lots of lies, and at least one cover-up. But I can't tell you any details."

"Well, I hope it gets declassified soon, because it sounds like it would make a wonderful movie!"

"I wonder who would play me?" I replied.

"Hedy Lamarr would be perfect for you," said Ginnie. "Apparently, she is terrifyingly smart. Joy might get Bacall."

"That would be okay," I said, "but I was hoping you'd say Hepburn."

"Knowing Hollywood, they'd probably cast Bogart," said Joy, ruefully. "And I'd just be his girl sidekick who makes eyes at him the whole movie."

"This is all turning out to be a bit sad," said Ginnie. "Let's go for a walk and do some window-shopping!"

I knew it wouldn't be Joy's idea of fun, but I deduced that Ginnie needed the distraction. We gathered our coats, hats, and purses, and headed for the door.

"Wait, did you pay?" asked Joy.

"They'll put it on my account," replied Ginnie, airily. Nobody seemed to be pursuing us or urgently waving a check, so I had to assume this was normal for people like Ginnie.

Outside, the street was busier than the Lounge had been. The celebrities might be able to migrate to warmer climes, but the ordinary folks were stuck here for the winter. Not that the winter in LA was much to complain about, especially compared to Ohio. It was certainly the rainy season, but temperatures rarely got below sixty. People were swaddled in raincoats, but their scarves were mostly for display.

As we exited the hotel, Ginnie turned away the doorman with the slightest shake of the head before he could ask if we needed a taxi. I felt like rich people—along with the people whose jobs were to keep rich people's lives moving along smoothly—had an entire secret language of gestures unknown to the rest of us. We turned right and headed down to the corner where we could cross Sunset Boulevard and walk through the park.

We waited at the corner for the lights to change, then another couple of seconds because none of us trusted LA drivers to always stop on red. We had crossed two lanes of impatient traffic when suddenly, Joy's arm went around my waist, spinning me backwards. Before I could react, a car bolted out of the left-turn lane and shot into the intersection. It grazed Joy's hip and smacked forcefully into the man to her right. He had taken one more step than us, and the car's right fender knocked him a couple of feet sideways and sent him sprawling to the pavement, where he landed face down. The car barreled on and smacked its dented fender into another car crossing the intersection, the impact turning it sideways. The driver put his foot down, spinning the tires for a moment before they grabbed the pavement. Then he pointed the car down Rodeo Drive, and disappeared into the traffic. The whole incident had taken no more than thirty seconds.

"You okay?" Joy asked me. Ginnie was gripping my arm tightly, her face ashen.

"Thanks to you, yes," I replied. I looked over at the man still lying on the pavement, and tried not to think that it could just as easily have been me. He groaned loudly, but all of his limbs seemed to be moving. A crowd was gathering around him.

"What about you, Joy?" I asked.

"He just brushed me. Did you get the license plate?"

"Yes. And the make, model, and year. Did either of you see the driver?"

Joy shook her head. "Just the back of his head. It was some guy wearing a trilby."

"Or a tall woman with a short haircut, wearing a man's hat," I added pedantically. I wasn't falling for that again.

I heard sirens approaching from a few blocks away.

"We should wait for the police and give them the details," I said.

"Okay," said Ginnie, "and after that, I'm going to need another drink." She still looked pale, but at least she had loosened her grip on my arm.

An ambulance was first to arrive. The driver and attendant manhandled the injured man onto a stretcher and loaded him into the back of their vehicle. I caught a glimpse of his eyes as they passed. He looked dazed and confused.

The police arrived a few minutes after—a couple of officers in a patrol car. One was old and one was young, and I wondered if they always paired them up like that. I made a mental note to ask Eddie. They started taking statements from bystanders, and eventually found their way around to us. Joy went first.

"The car was in the left turn lane, but hung back a couple of car lengths instead of pulling forward, which seemed odd to me," she told the older officer. "Then the driver floored it. I was able to pull Dot out of the way. The guy to our right got clipped pretty hard."

"He's at the hospital," I added. "But he might not remember much. I think he was concussed."

"Can you describe the car at all?" asked the cop.

"A brown 1940 Pontiac Deluxe Six Sport Coupe," I told him. I gave him the license plate too. He gave me a look that I was very familiar with and which I had learned to interpret more or less as, 'who do you think you're kidding?' Then I watched him write on his report, 'witness identified a four-door sedan.'

"No, two-door," I said. "The Sport Coupe has only two doors."

He smirked. "Ma'am, I've been doing this a long time. Everybody thinks they remember more details than they really do. It just mixes things up if we take every witness at face value. So I'll just write down what we know for sure."

I sighed. "I understand, but I'm not 'everybody.' You're looking for a coupe, which is a lot less common than the sedan."

He still didn't write it down. "Thank you, ma'am," was all he said.

"I understand why you don't believe me," I said, as calmly as I could manage. "It's not my first time. Please call Detective Ramirez in homicide. He'll explain it to you. Or if you prefer, I'll call him and he will let you know himself. I know your badge number, it won't be hard for him to find you." I hoped that didn't come across like I was threatening to have Eddie pull rank on him. I just wanted the driver to be found.

He glared at me for a few seconds, then crossed out what he'd written and instead wrote 'witness claims to have seen a brown 1940 Pontiac Deluxe Six Sports Coupe.'

"And the license plate," I added.

He gave me another glare, and wrote that down too. He probably still didn't believe me, but maybe somebody who read his report would.

We made our way back to the Polo Lounge. The staff pretended not to notice that we'd left barely thirty minutes before. Ginnie drained her first Rob Roy before she'd even lit a cigarette, but took her second more slowly. I barely touched my Manhattan. I was thinking about how Barbara had died, and what we had just witnessed, and my head was filled with disturbing thoughts and connections I didn't want to be true. I waited impatiently until, as best I could tell, Ginnie had recovered her equilibrium.

"Ginnie, are you going to be okay?" I asked.

"I'm fine," Ginnie replied. "That was all very alarming, but I'm settled now." There was that *sang froid* her expensive schools had taught her.

"If you're sure, we need to get back to the office," I said.

We made our way out to the front and the doorman whistled up a taxi for Ginnie.

"If you need us later, call the office," I told her. "If we're not there, we're probably at Jack's. You know you're welcome to join us if you need a stiffener."

"And you don't mind slumming," said Joy with a smile.

"Thank you," said Ginnie. "If I don't feel like being alone, I will definitely do that."

Joy and I rode the Red Line back to our office. She apparently intuited that I didn't want to talk until we were alone. Once we were settled inside with coffee and cigarettes, Joy pulled up a chair on the other side of my desk.

"What's so urgent?" she said.

"I have a strong suspicion that hit-and-run was no accident," I replied.

Joy stared at me for a couple of seconds before responding. "You think you were targeted. And you think it's connected to the Paperclip case," she said.

"We need to make a phone call to Morgan." I pulled out the card he had given me and dialed his number while Joy went back to her desk and picked up her extension. Morgan picked up on the third ring.

"Dot Stone here," I said. "We have some news we think you'd be interested in."

There was a brief pause filled only by crackling on the line.

"Sure," he replied. "I do owe the two of you a coffee."

"How about something stronger?" I asked.

"I guess I could do that. It's almost five already. Where?"

"Can you come to us this time?" I asked. I gave him the address for Jack's.

An hour later, the three of us were sat around a table, drinks in front of us. Morgan's first reaction on opening the door to Jack's had been a lot like mine. Before your eyes adjust to the dark, your nose is assaulted by the smell of stale beer and cheap floor cleaner. As your sight improves, you realize that the furniture is heavy and coarse and well-worn. Then you take in the size, just a dozen tables and a couple of booths. The last thing you notice is that the barman is glaring impatiently at you, wondering why you haven't ordered yet. It was easy to dismiss the place, as I had done the first time I'd come in here. It took a second look to realize that Jack's was defined by its patrons, not its decor. And its patrons were good people.

Morgan joined at us at our table with a beer in hand, and we got right down to business, telling him about the afternoon's near-miss.

"So you think that this wasn't an accident," said Daniel. "You think somebody tried to run you down."

"Yes, just like Barbara," I replied. "Doesn't that strike you as more than coincidence?"

"The guy had stopped his car a couple of car lengths back from the intersection, like he wanted to give himself a run-up," said Joy. "He hit the gas just as we were about to step in front of him."

Daniel gave that some thought. "Yes, that does sound odd. But why would you be a target? Surely it can't be the case, it's closed."

"Did you put your report in?" I asked.

"Yes, Monday evening. Your report was so detailed, it didn't take me long to write mine."

"And you included your recommendation to keep the investigation open?"

"Yes, but I know they're not going to. It's just my way of putting on the record that I dissent from the decision."

"Okay, I have a theory about this. Let's look at the timeline. I arrived at the TDL on Sunday the 9th, and on Tuesday morning, I asked you to look into Lewis and Ali. I assume you wrote that down somewhere?"

"Of course, I logged the information requests. Then I locked the log in my safe."

"Who would know about the requests?"

"Just Mary McCardy, our secretary. She submitted the requests for me. Why?"

"That night, Caroline was attacked."

"Oh," said Joy. "You think Caroline wasn't the target. You think that was meant for you."

"Yes," I replied. "We're about the same height and figure, and it's possible she left the officers' club not long after I did. Somebody could easily have mistaken her for me in the dark."

"Do you think they intended to hurt you enough that you'd have to leave?" asked Daniel. "Or was it just supposed to be a warning?"

"Unclear. And without knowing whether they said anything to Caroline, I don't think we can ever know. Now, I talked to Joy about my theories on Wednesday. Did she share those with you?"

"Yes, she called me and briefed me. That's protocol. I logged it and locked the log away as before. So what?"

"So the very next day, I got a Valentine's Day card with something that sounded very much like a threat. Are you starting to see a pattern?"

"Go on," he said, his brow deeply furrowed.

"Okay. Then on Monday morning, I called you and we talked about Lewis again, and I asked you to look into Schäfer. I assume that also went into the log and into the safe. And the next day, the operation was shut down. Every time I reported some progress to you, I got some pushback."

"There's a lot of supposition going on there," Joy pointed out.

"True, but either we've got a narrative that makes sense of it all, or we've got a jumble of nonsense. Let's play out the narrative for now."

"Alright," said Daniel. "Supposing this is correct, it raises a major question. How did they know what progress you were making and what you were asking me to look into?"

"You said earlier that only your secretary would know when you made official information requests. If she is the inside leak, that would account for some of it."

Daniel leaned back in his chair, his face stony. "I would have to see something a lot more convincing than a string of coincidences before I would suspect Mary. Besides, there's a lot in my logs that Mary wouldn't have seen. Nor anybody else for that matter."

"Not even your director sees them?"

"Not until your assignment was complete. We're deeply protective of undercover assets. So I have no idea how anybody would know what progress you had made. Based on opportunity alone, I'd want to arrest me."

"Okay, let's set aside McCardy for the moment," said Joy. She gave me a look that I didn't know what to make of, but she later explained was supposed to mean "cool it with this line of speculation". How anybody is supposed to get that from a facial expression is a mystery to me.

"Still, somebody knew things that you wrote and locked away," I said. "That makes me worry about the trustworthiness of anybody who had access to it."

"Nobody else has the combination, not even Wardour," said Daniel tersely. He seemed to be getting a little angry.

"Could somebody have cracked it?" I didn't know much about breaking into safes, but I wanted to pursue this thought to its logical conclusion.

"That seems very unlikely to me. I have an extremely secure safe, not the kind the average homeowner might have. And if you're insinuating that one of my colleagues…"

Daniel was definitely heated now.

"I can think of another version of events," said Joy, interrupting. "Maybe the leak is at the other end."

"How?" asked Daniel.

"Could the phone booths back at the army base be bugged? If so, somebody might know every word you and Dot exchanged. Me and Dot too. There could be bugs in the booths, or even in the phones themselves. I read that they make them really small these days."

"That's possible," Daniel said. "Somebody would have to listen to a lot of unrelated calls to get to the good stuff, but it seems a lot more likely to me than either a colleague betraying us, or somebody opening my safe. I really wish you would drop that and focus on something more credible."

He took a long draft of his beer. He looked slightly calmer.

And then something that had been nagging at me bubbled up. "By the way," I said, "did you send a limo to pick me up at the airport?"

"No," said Daniel. "Why do you ask?"

"It's another thread I need to tug on. It's probably nothing, but I'll let you know."

"So what's next? I still can't do anything officially. And I don't want you two to do anything dangerous."

"I don't either," I said. "But we need to figure out who tried to kill us. And why."

"Listen, I have to get going. And I'm writing none of this down. Let me know if you learn anything. And above all, be careful."

"We will."

We watched him out the door.

"That phone bug idea of yours has a lot of merit," I said. "It also makes me think, if there's an insider involved, the phones at this end could be bugged too."

"Yes, both Daniel's, and ours," replied Joy. "That definitely sounds like an OSS kind of thing to do. But how would we check? I don't know what a phone tap looks like. You?"

"No, me neither," I replied. "I was sort of hoping that you might have read about them in those crime magazines of yours."

"They mention them from time to time, but never describe them. But I do have one idea. Sam has been at this a lot longer than we have, maybe he knows what to look for."

Sam had been a cop for enough years to retire on a full pension, and had been a private detective for another ten years after that. Of all of our friends, he was definitely our best bet.

"Good thought. And we need to be careful what we say on the phone from now on, until we know for sure."

"I need to unwind after all that. Let's get a drink with the boys," said Joy, hooking her thumb towards the clutch of cab drivers at the back of the room. I squeezed in alongside Madge and waited for a break in the conversation. I wasn't quite done with work yet.

"Madge, I need to ask a favor," I said. "We're looking for a car. Brown, 1940 Pontiac Deluxe Six Sports Coupe. Can you ask the drivers to keep an eye out for it, and call it in if they spot it?" I wrote down the license plate for her.

"Of course," she replied. "Should I ask what it's about?"

"Better if you don't know," I said. "But tell them not to approach it, just call it in. The driver might very well be dangerous. And there's another thing you might be able to help me with. Do you know much about limo companies?"

"A little. Sometimes they'll call me if they are short and need to borrow a driver."

"How many limo companies are there in the city?"

"Lots. Probably dozens, most of them unlicensed. It's not like it's a hard business to get into. You just need a nice car and a uniform."

"Darn. Can you think of a way I could identify what company a driver was working for?"

"Did he have a badge on his lapel?"

I closed my eyes and pictured the scene.

"Yes. He had a metal pin of an eagle, painted red, white, and blue."

"I know them. Believe it or not, they are called American Eagle Limo. They'll be in the Yellow Pages."

"Thanks, Madge. I owe you. Again."

After that, I tried to push thoughts of work out of my head so I could enjoy the remainder of the evening.

Chapter Fourteen

When I got to the office that morning, I was surprised to see that Joy was already there and had made coffee.

"So, about last night…" she said. "Daniel was really mad at you. I don't know if you picked that up."

"I did get that he was annoyed, eventually," I replied. "He seems determined not to believe that there is a leak coming from inside the Bureau. But I don't understand why he refuses to follow where the evidence leads. Isn't that what a good analyst should do?"

"You don't get how personal this is for him," explained Joy, patiently. "These are his closest colleagues. They probably had some serious wartime experiences together. It's hard for people to just set aside that trust, especially when the evidence is so circumstantial."

"And his refusal to consider that the safe might be insecure?"

"It's all part of it. If he accepts that his safe is crackable, he has to consider that one of his colleagues might be cracking it. And he really does not want to go down the line of thinking."

I was silent for a minute, drinking my coffee, and trying to fit Daniel's emotions into the rational pattern I was seeing emerge.

Joy interrupted my reverie. "Think about this way. How would you feel if a customer came in here and accused me of deliberately sabotaging one of our cases?" she asked.

"You're right," I said. "I'd need to see cast iron proof before I was willing to even consider the possibility. And I think that means we're going to have to give Daniel the same if we're going to budge him."

"You have something in mind, don't you?"

"I have an idea. Do you mind if I keep it to myself until it's a plan?"

Joy sighed heavily. "You know, whenever you do that, it's usually something dangerous. And you think I'm going to hate it."

I nodded. She was right on both counts.

I picked up my phone and called Eddie to see if he could take an hour off. He said that if nobody died, he could meet me for coffee at eleven.

I rode the Red Line over there and was seated five minutes before eleven. Eddie arrived five minutes after, but I forgave him. I was lucky to get him at all on a day when he was working. I reflected that, in fact, I was lucky to get him in general. He was intelligent, kind, generous, and thoughtful, and on top of that, pretty darn good looking. And the things that he said he liked most about me—that I was smart, resourceful, and independent—were exactly the things I most wanted to believe about myself.

Once he was settled with a coffee in front of him, I told him about the incident with the car.

"Yeah, I got a call from the patrolman, wanting to know if you were legit," he said. "He sounded pretty skeptical. I told him that if you said you got the make and model, he could trust it. I hope that helped."

"Thanks," I replied. "I don't suppose there's any chance you can take over the case as an attempted homicide, can you?"

"It's unlikely, but I could try. I would need to pitch a case to my lieutenant. Can you tell me why you're so convinced it wasn't just a routine traffic incident?"

I inhaled the aroma of my coffee while I gave that some thought. "No, I don't think I can. Everything convincing is classified."

"Sorry, I guess we're stuck then. The best I can do is keep an eye on the case and ask for updates."

"I'd appreciate that," I told him. "I have another request. It's an even longer shot, though. Do you happen to know any safecrackers? No surprise, but I can't say why."

"Is it at least something legal?"

I hesitated, carefully formulating my reply. "I'm not planning to steal anything, if that's what you mean"

"That sounded like a non-denial," said Eddie, perceptively.

I sighed. "You're right. I shouldn't have involved you in this. I do have a backup plan, but I would have preferred not to go there."

"Do I want to know what it is?"

"Absolutely not," I said. I picked up my cup and hid behind my coffee.

I turned the conversation to what movie we would see that evening, assuming, as Eddie pointed out, somebody didn't ruin our plans by getting themselves killed in the meantime.

Eddie headed back to his office, and a sat a little while longer. My next phone call was going to be difficult, and I rehearsed in my mind how the conversation might go. I did this a lot, even though the conversations almost never went the way I had imagined them. Still, it helped me to manage my anxiety. Once I knew what I wanted to say, I rode a streetcar over to Jack's. I didn't want a drink, but the guy I was planning to call would not be happy if I did it from a phone that I suspected might be tapped.

I settled myself in Jack's phone booth and lit a Kool to help settle myself, then picked up the phone and dialed a number from memory. On the fourth ring, a woman's voice answered.

"Could you see if Mr. Accardo is available?" I said in my best bookshop voice. "Please tell him it's Dot Stone." The phone made a hefty clunk as if the handset had been dropped on a table.

Accardo and I had a history. He was a well-connected mobster from Chicago who had brought his business to LA. I was under no illusion about the fact that his dealings were all illegal, and sometimes required threats and violence. However, he tried to keep those to a minimum, considering them inefficient. He liked to think of himself as a businessman with a code of honor, and that vanity was something I could work with. It was obvious to me that LA would never entirely rid itself of the mob, so I had reconciled myself to the thought that if we were going to have organized crime, it should at least be well-organized.

Accardo came on the line. "Miss Stone, it's been a while. I want to thank you for the thing in the place with the guy. I owe you for that."

Accardo talked in ciphers like that all the time, as though he thought that the Feds were listening to all his calls. In fairness, they probably were. The 'guy' was a mafioso named Lorenzo Vincenti who had turned informant against rival gangsters, including Accardo. The 'place' was Las Vegas. And the 'thing' was getting Vincenti arrested for murder, which had made me and Joy a lot safer, and incidentally meant that Accardo owed me a favor. A lot of Accardo's business seemed to operate on an unwritten ledger of favors granted, owed, and repaid.

"You're welcome," I said. "And I do have a request for a favor of my own."

"We should meet," he said. Apparently, he was feeling even more cautious than usual. And as quickly as that, my carefully prepared conversation was in the trash can.

He told me to be at Hollenbeck Park in an hour and to meet him at the eastern end of the bridge over the lake. As always, I knew he was not asking for a debate about the time and place.

I arrived a few minutes early, as is my habit, and stood alone by the bridge. After a couple of minutes, I heard footsteps crunching on the gravel path, and turned to see Accardo coming up behind me.

"Walk," he said, and we followed the path alongside the lake. I tried my best to seem relaxed, but there was something about this man that always felt menacing to me, even here in this quiet lakeside park where I had no logical reason to feel afraid. Perhaps it was simply knowing what he was capable of if he ever decided that his business was better off with me dead rather than alive. I guessed that was one of the things that made him so good at his job.

I had thought carefully about how to word my request in a way that could not be used against him if somebody were somehow eavesdropping. I briefly wondered what range parabolic microphones had these days, then snapped my attention back to the present task.

"I am considering buying a safe for my office," I said. "However, I'm concerned about how secure they really are. I wondered if you might be able to recommend a security expert who could examine the model I have in mind. And it needs to be somebody who will respect my confidentiality completely."

"Where would this examination take place?" asked Accardo.

"In the office of a friend who owns the model I'm interested in," I replied. Strictly speaking, every word of that was true.

A rowing boat came up alongside us, passed, and splashed off into the distance. Only when the sound of its oars sitting the water was almost gone did Accardo speak again.

"If I do this for you, we'll be even. Are you sure this is the favor you want to ask of me?"

I thought about that for several seconds. Accardo was a powerful man, and there many strings he could pull on somebody's behalf. A part of my mind wanted to think about what I might have to do for Accardo if I ever needed another favor, but I didn't have time for that. Right now, I needed to figure out who wanted me dead, and this seemed like the only way to unblock Daniel's obstruction.

"It's not the one I want to ask," I replied, "but it is the one I need to ask."

"Fair enough. I know a guy, and he owes me a favor. I'll talk to him and ask him to call your office." When Accardo said 'ask', he generally meant 'tell.' "Turn around and walk back the way you came," he told me, and continued his walk.

I walked back to the bridge, crossed over the lake, and exited the park on St. Louis Street. Only then did it occur to me that I should have asked Joy before using up all our credit on this request.

By the time I got back to the office, Joy had returned from the tail job she had been on that morning. I began to explain what I had been up to, and was about to ask her forgiveness for calling on Accardo without talking it over with her, but the phone interrupted us. I picked up.

"Miss Stone? Our mutual friend said to give you a call." The rasp on the other end was almost, but not quite, a whisper.

This was not a conversation I wanted to risk having tapped.

"I'm sorry, but I can't talk right now. Can I call you back in a few minutes?"

"Of course," he said. He gave me his number and hung up.

"Want to fill me in?" Joy asked.

"That man is going to try to crack Daniel's safe for us."

She raised her eyebrows and opened her eyes wide.

"You think Daniel is going to let a safecracker into his office just because you ask him nicely?"

"I wasn't planning to ask. And I'm going to leave him a note to prove we did it."

Joy stared at me for several seconds. "That is the most cockeyed idea I've ever heard from you. And I've heard some doozies."

"I know it's dangerous, but the only way I'm going to get him to believe that the traitor is inside his bureau is to show him that somebody there had access to his notes. And the only way to do that is to prove it can be cracked."

"It's insane, but I won't be able to talk you out of it, will I?"

I left her to hold down the office while I walked over to Jack's to call Accardo's friend back. My call was picked up after one ring.

"Yes?" said the same raspy whisper as before.

"This is Miss Stone. Sorry about that, but I had to go to a different phone."

"I understand entirely," he replied.

If he dealt with Accardo regularly, he probably did.

"Thank you for calling so promptly. That was much faster than I expected."

"When our mutual friend says to call, I get right on the horn."

"Of course. And do you have a name?"

He paused. "You can call me Tony."

"Alright then. Anyway, yes, I have a small job for you."

"A box job, right? What's a shamus need with a lay like that?"

I wished Joy were here to translate. She had picked up a lot of this argot from the detective stories and true crime magazines she read when things were quiet in the office.

"If that means opening a safe, then yes. I can't tell you whose it is, but it's inside the Federal building."

"What about the B&E? I only do safes."

"I've got that handled myself," I said. I waited for some pushback on that, and was surprised when none came.

"Soup job or on the q.t.?"

I was starting to think that this man thought he was auditioning for a bit part in a gangster movie. Actually, that was true of a lot of people in LA, and it was one of the most annoying things about living here.

"I don't know what that means," I told him, my brow creased.

"Explosives or quiet?"

"The latter."

"Where and when?"

"An office in the Federal Building. As soon as possible."

"I can do tonight," he said. "Two in the morning is the best time. Everybody is dopey around then, even the cops on night shift."

"You don't want to know whose office we're breaking into?" I asked.

"Nope. Your business is your business, I always say. It doesn't pay to ask questions you don't need to know the answer to."

We arranged a meeting spot across the street from the Federal Building. I hung up and walked back to the office.

I explained my plan to Joy. She reiterated that I was taking a massive risk.

"What's the alternative?" I asked. "Sit around waiting for the guy in the car to try to murder us again? Or hope that the LAPD can track down somebody who is probably an agent trained in eluding capture, assuming the cops even care about a routine hit-and-run?"

Joy sighed heavily. "I wish I had something better," she said. "But if you're going to do this, I'm going to back you up. I'll be your lookout, okay?"

The rest of the day dragged by with routine work. Joy and I had dinner at a nearby diner, then I headed home for whatever rest I could manage before dressing in my black outfit and heading out again.

I met Tony as arranged. He looked to be around forty years old, with salt-and-pepper hair, and was dressed in faded jeans, a dark blue button-down shirt without a collar, and loafers. He had a flat cap on his head and in his hand, he carried a Gladstone bag which I assumed contained the tools of his trade. He was as pale as you might expect of a man who didn't go out in daylight much. If he were in a police line-up, even if you had never seen him before, you would pick him out merely on principle. If he didn't have a nickname like 'the Fingers,' there was no justice in this world.

He looked me up and down. "Are you trying to get arrested?" he asked derisively.

"What do you mean?" I asked in reply.

"You look like you dressed as a burglar for Hallowe'en."

"Sorry. Look, can we just get this done?"

We approached the Federal Building. The front door yielded quickly to my lock picks. I assumed there would be greater challenges inside. We took the stairs to the third floor, and I led Tony to the door of the offices Daniel and his colleagues were using. I set to work with my picks and it was immediately obvious that this was a more serious lock than I was used to. It had seven pins, and the tolerances were much tighter. Loose tolerances are a lockpicker's friend. Tony waited patiently as three minutes went by before the pins finally fell into place. I opened the door and led him down the corridor. We quickly found Daniel's office. His safe was in plain sight, embedded into the wall.

Tony smiled. "It's a Mecum Platinum. This shouldn't take long," he said.

At that moment, a car horn sounded outside, long and loud. I looked out the window and saw two police patrol cars pulling up across the far side of the plaza, their red beacon lights unmistakable even at a distance.

"We have to go," I said.

"Dammit," said Tony. "We must have tripped a silent alarm."

"We can go out the side, through the fire exit and down the fire escape," I said. We ran down the corridor, leaving the door unlocked. I hoped Daniel wouldn't connect that to me.

Tony got the exit first and shoved it open. Immediately an alarm blared out. There was nothing silent about it.

"This is a good time to not be dressed like a burglar," said Tony. He was probably right. With no reason to be quiet now, we clattered down the fire escape and ran across the grass to the street. A Red Star taxi was parked there, its motor idling.

"Get in!" shouted Joy.

"Come on," I said to Tony. "She's a friend."

"No thanks," he replied. "I'll take my chances on foot." And he set off walking, just an ordinary LA citizen out for a stroll at two in the morning.

Joy pulled away.

"Did it go okay?" she asked.

"No," I sighed. "Tony was just about to start when you sounded the horn. But thanks for the rescue, anyway."

"No problem. I saw the police beacons three blocks away. When they pulled up in front, I figured you'd have the smarts to go out the back way."

"I can't tell you how happy I was to see you there. And tomorrow morning, I am ditching this ridiculous outfit."

"By the way, when was the last time you broke in somewhere and got out cleanly?"

"So long ago I can't even remember," I grumbled.

Chapter Fifteen

The next day was Friday. I spent the morning with the Yellow Pages in one hand and my phone in the other, calling companies that sold safes, looking for one that had Daniel's model in stock. I finally landed on Truly Safe Co. The owner, Mr. Grady, said I could come by any time to take a look. I didn't tell him what I had in mind. My next call was to Tony. I asked him if he could meet me that afternoon, and gave him the address. He agreed, but said it would cost an extra five bucks.

Sam came over around noon to check our phone line. He took us down the alley next to our building to a green metal box attached to the wall. A bundle of wires ran from it up the side of the building, and then across to a nearby telephone pole. Sam popped the cover open to reveal an array of wires and screw terminals.

"This is the junction box for your line, and probably all the other stores until you get to the next alley," said Sam. "Each of these wire pairs is one telephone line."

"Do you see anything suspicious?" Joy asked.

"Yeah, right here. See how there's two pairs of wires connected to the same terminals? I'll bet that's your line. Somebody is listening in parallel to every call you make or receive." He put the cover back on the box.

I was amazed that it was so simple. No elaborate microphones hidden in handsets. It didn't even require getting inside our office.

"Why didn't you remove the tap?" asked Joy.

"Because then they'll know we're onto them," I said.

"That's right," said Sam. "Better to leave it in place. This way, you can ensure they only hear what you want them to hear."

"Surely they can't be listening the whole time, though?" said Joy.

"They probably have a wire recorder on the tap that activates every time the line is live. On the roof is most likely. Then they can check it from time to time, say, once a day. If they're really sophisticated, they might even have a radio up there relaying the calls to another location. That's how I'd do it."

We thanked Sam and he left. We went back inside.

"This certainly feels like OSS work," I said to Joy.

She nodded.

We took lunch at an Italian diner a couple of blocks away while I caught her up on my fallback plan for the safe. Joy had the spaghetti special and I had the macaroni and cheese. I only ever ate short pasta, because long pasta offered too much of a risk of flipping sauce onto my clothes. Joy had told me this was weird, but it seemed perfectly rational to me. Sometimes I wondered if she even liked spaghetti, or if she was just ordering it to tease me.

We arrived outside the Truly Safe Co. five minutes before three. According to the sign in the window, Truly was a family-owned Los Angeles institution since 1929, which was a very long time in California years. Tony was waiting. I introduced Joy.

"So now we're breaking into an empty safe in a safe store, in broad daylight?" asked Tony. "What's the gag?"

"I still need to know how secure that safe is, and now that we know the model, I was able to find one here. I can't say more."

"That's fine. Your business is your business, I always say."

We stepped inside and I glanced around the store. On one wall was a large selection of door and window locks, as well as various other devices I didn't immediately recognize. Behind the counter was a rack of key blanks. And on the other wall, there were rows of steel shelves, holding a dozen different models of small and medium-sized safes. I assumed that really big ones would be special order. Two Black men were standing behind the counter—an older man in perhaps his sixties, the other middle-aged, both tall and broad with the same high cheekbones.

"Mr. Grady?" I asked. They replied "Yes," in unison.

Father and son, I realized. Now that I looked closer, apart from some lines and some gray hair, the resemblance was strong.

"I'm Dot Stone, these are my colleagues, Joy D'Amico and Tony. I called earlier today."

"Yes," said the older man. "I remember. You're interested in the Mecum Platinum, right? An excellent choice."

"Yes, but before we buy, I would like to do a little security check. I want to see how quickly Tony can open it."

The Gradys looked at each other. I imagined this wasn't a request they heard very often.

"I assure you, the Platinum is very secure," said the younger Grady.

"Nevertheless," I replied. We stood silently, looking at each other for several seconds. I had found that simply saying nothing is a surprisingly effective tactic for getting people to concede.

"Very well," said the older Grady. "But if you damage it, you bought it."

The two Gradys lifted the safe off the shelf and set it on a table in the middle of the floor. It was cubical, about two feet on each side, with a combination lock and a handle on the door. It was identical in appearance to the one in Daniel's office.

"What do you think, Tony?" I asked.

"Duck soup," he replied.

Baffled, I looked at Joy. She sniggered.

"It just means 'easy'," she said.

The Gradys looked slightly offended, as if somebody had called their pet dog ugly.

"Now if you all would turn around for a couple of minutes," said Tony, "I don't like to be watched while I work. It makes me skittish."

We turned our backs. I checked my watch.

"Nice weather for this time of year," said the younger Grady.

"It looks like it might rain later," said the older.

"It usually does," said the younger.

"Quiet please," said Tony.

After that, we all stood in silence.

"Done," said Tony.

We turned around. The door of the safe stood open. Both Gradys looked deeply hurt now. The younger Grady examined the door closely, presumably looking for scratches, but came away satisfied. Or perhaps disappointed. I wasn't entirely sure.

"Three minutes and ten seconds," I said. I was impressed and disturbed in equal measure.

"Yeah, sorry," replied Tony. "It would have been a lot quicker if I'd used soup—uh, nitro—but you said quiet and he said no damage."

"Could you teach me to do that?" I asked. It looked like it would be even more fun than lockpicking.

He looked me up and down. "I could, but I'm not going to. I have a feeling you'd be really good at it, and I don't need the competition."

"Fair enough," I sighed.

"But if you need anything else opened, our mutual friend always knows how to reach me. And my rates are very reasonable."

"You know, we really do need a safe of our own," said Joy. "Since we're here, what do you recommend, Tony?"

"Honestly, this is as good as anything you're going to find in this size and budget," he replied. "It'll keep out regular burglars and can-openers just fine. I just happen to be very good at what I do."

"Can-openers?" I asked, baffled again.

"A low level safe-cracker," explained Joy, "as opposed to an expert like Tony here."

He smiled at the compliment.

"By the way, you're not just saying that so you can pay us a visit later?" she added.

"Nobody is dumb enough to rob an associate of our mutual friend," he replied.

I would have to ask Joy later whether that was a serious exchange or just friendly banter.

"Anyway, I have to take a bunk," said Tony.

He tipped his cap, slipped out the door, and disappeared.

"You're right about the safe," I told Joy. "We really should have something more secure than filing cabinets for sensitive documents."

We negotiated a price and arranged an installation date, which made the Gradys look a good deal happier. And we promised not to tell anybody about how easily Tony had opened it.

Another thought struck me. I described the strange lock I'd seen on Schäfer's case. "Have either of you seen anything like that?" I asked.

The younger Grady shook his head and looked at his father.

"No," he said. "It sounds like a cheap tamper-evident lock. We don't sell them, and I don't know of another store in LA that does. Our customers generally want to keep people out, not know when they've been in."

That was interesting. So it wasn't something civilians casually had access to. I realized that I hadn't asked Daniel about the lock, and added a mental note to do so the next time we talked to my stack of reminders.

Joy and I walked slowly back to the streetcar stop.

"We really need to talk to Daniel again, don't we?" she said.

"We do," I replied. "But we have one more stop to make first."

That stop was the office of the American Eagle Limo company. It was on the third floor of an unremarkable four-story brick office building with dirty windows and a jerky, rattling elevator with an operator to match that made me think about taking the stairs back down. Inside the small office, there was a single desk with a phone, an overflowing out-tray, and enough papers scattered over the surface to make me want to tidy up. Behind the desk there stood bookshelves filled with three-ring binders. The labels on the binders had been crossed out and written over many times.

And between the desk and the bookshelves sat a squirrely-looking man with thin hair and wire-rim glasses, wearing a tweed jacket patched at the elbows. He stood up to greet us. "Good afternoon, ladies," he said. "Can I help you?"

The voice was that of a confident, eager salesman, not at all what I had anticipated from his appearance. He would have made a great pitchman on radio.

"I had a ride booked with your company a couple of weeks ago," I replied, "and I'm trying to find out what happened."

"Oh! Did your driver not show up?"

"No, nothing like that. He was at the airport when I arrived. The thing is, I wasn't expecting a driver. So I was wondering if you could tell me who booked the car on my behalf?"

I gave him my name and the arrival date. He turned to the bookshelves and immediately plucked out one of the binders. Despite appearances, there apparently was some sort of system, and it was working for him. He flicked through until he found the page.

"Oh, I remember this. Manny was supposed to collect you, but then he saw you had a friend picking you up and he stormed off."

"Right, that was me," said Joy.

"He was pretty mad when he got back here, until I told him he was still getting paid. The name on the reservation is Jane Smith, if that means anything to you? Here's the phone number."

"How did she pay?" I asked.

"About an hour after I took the reservation, a courier arrived with an envelope of cash."

"One more thing," I said. "Where was the driver supposed to take me?"

"The parking garage of the Federal Building," he replied.

"Didn't that sound odd to you?"

"Not really. I just assumed that's where you'd left your car for your trip."

"Okay, thank you for your help."

Joy and I walked down to the first floor and outside.

"The Federal Building," she said. "Where the OSS office is located. Funny coincidence."

"Yes," I replied, "and I probably wouldn't have questioned it. I would have assumed that Daniel had brought our meeting forward."

"What's your guess?" said Joy.

"I'll bet that phone number is as fake as Jane Smith. Worst case scenario, somebody from OSS was waiting for me there. And the moment the limo driver was gone, I'd have been bundled into a car, driven off, and never heard from again."

"Somebody really did not want your report reaching Daniel, giving cause to reopen the investigation."

"That's what I'm thinking. And when that failed, somebody tried to take me out more directly."

"This is some nasty business."

"And it's getting very hard to deny that somebody from OSS is involved."

Chapter Sixteen

We arranged to meet Daniel at Jack's that evening. It felt like a safe place for us to speak in secret. We knew all the regulars by sight, and it wasn't the kind of bar that people casually dropped into. A stranger here would be as obvious as a stripper at a church service, as Joy colorfully put it. Drinks and cigarettes in hand, we arranged ourselves around a table.

I told Daniel what we had learned at the Truly Safe Co. He didn't need to know about my aborted visit to his office.

"Our man was clearly an expert," I told him, "but it really is possible that somebody with comparable skill was reading your reports if they had access to your office."

"And then there's the business with the limo," added Joy, "and the tap on our phones."

"I hate to admit it," said Daniel, "but it's becoming very hard to deny that it was an insider. Our office has very sophisticated and well-hidden alarms, and for an outsider to get in without triggering them, he would need to know they were there."

I wondered if he knew that somebody had triggered the alarm last night. If so, he had an impressive poker face. He took a long draw of beer and contemplated the off-white wall of the bar for a minute or more.

"It's not just the betrayal itself," he said eventually. His hangdog expression spoke volumes, even to me. "It's what it says about the integrity of the whole organization. Even if we find one traitor, who's to say how many more

Russian agents there might be?" He stared into his beer while his cigarette burned down unsmoked.

"We need to talk candidate traitors," he said. "And once again, what I'm telling you here could end up with me being tried for a long list of offenses."

"Understood," I replied. "Let's start with the two people closest to you, with the most opportunity to access your safe. Wardour and McCardy. Who has means and motive?"

"Okay. Wardour is about five years older than me, so say forty. He's been with the OSS since the very beginning, I believe, when the Brits were helping us get it up and running. Before the war, he was some sort of language professor."

"That doesn't sound like much of a background for a special operations type," I said.

"OSS recruits came from all over. The service only cared about individual capability, not what you did before."

"What kind of training would he have had? Safe cracking doesn't sound like something you'd learn for a job in research and analysis."

"Well, there's the thing. Before he came to Research, Wardour was in SI branch."

"What's SI?" asked Joy.

Daniel seemed to make a habit of forgetting that the rest of us were not fluent in the jargon of his organization.

"Secret Intelligence. They were the ones who conducted intelligence gathering in the field. They were trained in all kinds of things: codes—both using and breaking; disguise and concealment; radio and communications; handling other agents; weapons use; and hand-to-hand combat. A lot more besides. Lock picking and breaking into safes very likely figured in the curriculum."

I tried to reconcile that resumé with the slightly overweight, rather seedy man I had met.

"That certainly sounds like the means," I said. "And not just for breaking into your safe, but for running the whole operation."

"The other thing about SI is that they looked down on all the other branches. They called the operations people 'bang-bang boys'. And we were considered desk-bound pencil-pushers."

"Then why did he transfer?" asked Joy. "It doesn't make sense."

"He had some sort of bad experience on an operation. The kind of thing an agent doesn't want to talk about, and nobody with any sense asks about. He couldn't work in the field any longer. So they put him behind a desk. It was either that or leave the service entirely."

It was a story I was familiar with. Some men came back from the war untouched. Others came back with visible wounds. And others came back with wounds nobody else could see, wounds that might never heal.

"Okay, so we definitely have opportunity and very likely means," said Joy. "What about motive?"

"There you've got me, I'm afraid. I know nothing of his personal life. If he has a family, he's never mentioned it. Or any kind of life outside the office, for that matter."

"Dot and I made a list. Money, sex, pride, and envy were at the top. Your basic deadly sins. Any of those make sense?"

"Not immediately. Except maybe pride? Perhaps he misses the edge of field ops. He certainly resents being deskbound. It's hard to think that would be enough to go over to the other side, but it's all I've got for now."

"Alright. Let's talk about your secretary, Mary."

"Mary McCardy. Technically she's Wardour's secretary, as I mentioned before, but she does admin work for the whole team. She's in her twenties and single—or at least, doesn't wear a ring. She comes to work at nine, leaves at five, works reliably in between. I have no idea where she goes when she's not at the office. She's not exactly eager to be friends with her colleagues, and doesn't hide the fact that she doesn't like the work. She's been with us for a year or so, but I don't know what she did before. That's all pretty useless, isn't it?"

"She doesn't have obvious skills for cracking a safe, but people are full of surprises," said Joy, with a sideways glance at me. "Let's not rule her out. But for now, let's focus on Wardour. Ideas?"

Before anybody could answer, we were interrupted by Jack. "Joy, Madge is on the blower for you!" he shouted across the room.

We'd been so deep in conversation, I hadn't even heard the phone ring. Joy went over to the bar and Jack stretched the cord across to her. She listened for a brief minute before speaking.

"Great," she said. "Can you call the local cops and let them know? We'll be there in ten minutes." She came back to the table.

"We caught a break. One of the cabbies spotted the coupé parked in an alleyway over in West LA. Madge is letting us borrow a cab to go over there."

That was good news. It would take us hours to get all the way out there on streetcars.

By the time we arrived, the police were already on the scene. They had set a barricade across the alley and two bored uniformed officers were standing next to it, presumably to make sure nobody stole it. The alley ran between the windowless walls of two warehouses, which were perhaps four stories tall. The light was already fading, and the alley was in shadow.

To my surprise, Eddie's car was also here, parked behind the police cruiser. We walked over to the barricade and peered into the alley.

"Something you need, miss?" said one of the cops. His tone had all the usual contempt for civilians gawping at a crime scene.

I flashed my P.I. badge. It didn't impress him.

"Is Detective Martinez around? He wanted me down here," I asked. It was certainly possible that was true. One of the things I had learned in this business was to lie creatively, but my instinct was that the best lies sailed as close to the truth as possible.

The cop turned his head and shouted over his shoulder, "Detective! There's a private dick here to see you!"

The passenger-side door of the Pontiac opened and Eddie stepped out. He caught sight of me, waved, and sauntered over to the barrier.

"Miss Stone," he said. "Nice to see you. You too, Miss D'Amico." I assumed the formality was for the benefit of the two uniformed cops. He looked at Daniel and raised his eyebrows. "And this is…?"

"Our client. Sorry, can't say more than that," I replied.

"Understood."

"How are you here? I thought you couldn't get involved in a hit-and-run?"

"There's a dead guy in the driver's seat. So now it's officially a homicide. My lieutenant knew you were involved, so when the uniforms called it in, he let me take it. You two swing some weight around our squad room, after the business last year with Vincenti."

"Any witnesses?"

"I have a couple of uniforms canvassing the area, but I'm not expecting much. It's basically warehouses on this block and the next one. So unless somebody happened to be making a pickup or a delivery, it's pretty much deserted."

"Any clues in the car?" asked Joy.

"Not so far," replied Eddie. "Do you want to take a look? The stiff doesn't have any ID, but maybe you'll recognize him if he really was targeting one of you. I should warn you, there's some blood, but you've seen much worse."

I caught the two cops exchanging looks of surprise at that. They stepped aside and let Joy and I pass through.

"Not you, sir," Eddie said to Daniel. "Sorry."

We walked over to the Pontiac and peered inside. Eddie pointed his flashlight at the corpse. The face was pale, slack, open-eyed, and familiar.

"I know the guy," I said. "Lieutenant Ted Lewis, US Army Air Forces. He's assigned to—or, was assigned to—the base at Wright Field. Dayton, Ohio."

Apparently, this case didn't want to let go of me any more than I wanted to let go of it.

"Is this related to the undercover job you can't talk about?"

"It is."

We walked back up to the barricade. "It's Lewis," I told Daniel.

"How did he die?" he asked.

"We'll have to wait for the coroner to be sure," said Eddie, "but judging by the location of the blood, it looks like he was stabbed in the base of the skull."

Daniel turned white.

"What's up?" asked Joy.

"That's an OSS technique for silently killing a sentry. Done correctly, it immediately paralyzes the victim so they can't struggle. They can't even cry out."

"Great," Eddie said with a hefty sigh. "An army officer for a victim and a spook for the attacker. The bureaucracy on this is going to kill me."

I had long ago learned that one of the ways Eddie dealt with the relentless parade of corpses and killers in his job was a very dry sense of humor.

"Ask the coroner to look for a wound made by a very thin stiletto blade. That's the OSS weapon of choice for this kind of thing."

"So wait, the killer would have to be in the seat behind the driver?" said Joy.

"It's a two door. How did he get in there?" asked Eddie. "If they rode together, it would have been very weird not to ride side by side up front. The guy's not running a cab service here."

"Maybe the killer held a gun on him and forced him to drive out here?" said Joy.

"I don't think so," said Daniel. "If you're going to a stiletto into precisely the right spot like that, you need to take your victim completely by surprise. It's not something you can do right if somebody is moving around. If you're being forced to drive at gunpoint and you think you're going to die at the end of it, surely you fight back at some point. Like when your enemy puts down their gun to pull out their knife, for instance."

"There's no sign of any struggle in the car," said Eddie. "The victim might as well have been asleep when it happened."

I stared into the distance for a couple of moments. "So the killer needs to get Lewis somewhere isolated, and didn't force him to drive there at gunpoint. Instead, he calls Lewis and asks to meet here, at the end of an alley, out of sight in a quiet neighborhood. That means it's somebody Lewis trusts, or at least knows. But before Lewis can get to his car, the murderer slips inside and conceals himself behind the front seat. He waits until they arrive here, then kills Lewis before he has any idea he has a passenger."

"That runs a big risk of being spotted in the back seat," Joy pointed out.

"Our killer's smart, so assume it was night. And he's well concealed in the back of the car. That would also make this an even better location for the kill. I'll bet this alley is pitch black after dark. Any idea on the time of death?"

"We'll have to wait for the coroner for an official answer on that too," said Eddie. "But based on the lividity, I'd say at least eight hours ago. That's possibly consistent with your theory. I'll also tell SID to check the back of the car thoroughly, but if we're dealing with a trained operative, I doubt we'll find anything."

"What's SID?" asked Joy.

"Scientific Investigation Division," I explained. "Scientists, fingerprint specialists, forensic photographers, that kind of thing. It's amazing what they can tell from the traces left at a crime scene."

Eddie nodded. "Any thoughts on motive?" he asked. "Anybody who would want Lewis dead?"

"I can think of a couple, but they're in Dayton. Or at least, they were. Up until ten minutes ago, I thought Lewis was also in Dayton."

"And I assume you can't tell me who they are," said Eddie with a resigned shrug.

I looked at Daniel. "I think it's time you read Eddie in."

We gathered in an interview room back at Eddie's station. He latched the door and closed the blinds.

"Before we do this," said Daniel, "you need to know what you're signing up for. I crossed my Rubicon a while back, and Joy and Dot are already deep in. If I brief you, I'll be sharing classified information that I shouldn't tell and you shouldn't know. You can figure out for yourself the consequences if that comes to light."

"I understand," said Eddie. "Right now, I feel like I already know more than I should, but not enough to help. Better I get the whole ball of wax."

"Very well. My name is Daniel Morgan. I am an agent with the Office of Intelligence Research, part of the Department of State—quite possibly soon to be a disgraced former agent. We used to be part of OSS. I recruited Dot to investigate a suspected intelligence leak originating from a military research project at Wright Field, and she asked for Joy to be read in to support her."

"So that's where you were for two weeks," said Eddie. "No wonder you couldn't say anything."

"It was tough," I said. "There were so many things I wanted to pick your brain about."

Daniel proceeded to bring Eddie up to speed. He interrupted minimally for clarifications. It took around twenty minutes while we all sipped at weak, cold, bitter coffee and wished we were at Café del Sol.

"And that's the whole story?" said Eddie when Morgan finished. "What a mess."

"Here's another thing that strikes me," said Joy. "It seems weird to leave the car and the body over in West LA. They were sure to be found eventually. If it were me, I'd have driven the car over to Santa Monica and run it off a pier there. It's only another five miles."

"You have a theory about that?" asked Eddie.

"I think we were supposed to find it. There's a message. Somebody is saying to leave the investigation alone. And they are saying it very loud."

We all gave that some thought.

"Or we're all reading too much into it," I said. "Maybe the killer simply wasn't strong enough to move the body from the driver's seat. A small woman, for example."

I turned to Eddie. "Who do you like for it?" I asked. His instincts could be hugely valuable here.

"We're all thinking that one of Morgan's colleagues would obviously be favorite, since we know they're here in LA, and it fits the OSS training, right?" he replied. "But I don't see a motive. What about you?"

"I agree with you on all of that. On the other hand, if we're looking at people on the base, Reardon might finally have lost it with Lewis, but in terms of skill and technique, that seems like a very long shot. And if Hathaway were being blackmailed by Lewis, he might have decided to get out from under. Again, the skill required speaks against it unless Hathaway has a secret history with OSS."

"Let's cover all our bases, just in case. Daniel, any chance you can call Hathaway and find out whether anybody has left the base?"

"Sure," said Daniel. "But I'll need to borrow a phone. I'm no longer confident that the ones in my office are secure."

Eddie led Daniel to a private office. They returned ten minutes later.

"Hathaway is out of town on vacation, but I got his lieutenant," said Daniel. "The only other person not accounted for is Lewis, and he's AWOL. I didn't tell him we know where Lewis is. I don't know whose side he's on, and until I do, information asymmetry is our advantage."

"Anybody else think it's odd that Hathaway is out of town when Lewis is killed?" asked Eddie.

"Daniel, I don't suppose you know where he went?" I asked.

"Actually, I do," said Daniel. "Because he's responsible for security, he has to be reachable in an emergency. I told them this was an emergency."

"And?"

"Allegedly he's at Palm Springs, staying at La Quinta."

"That can't be right," said Joy. "La Quinta is a really ritzy joint. It's where the Hollywood crowd hang out."

"So how does a man with a captain's salary and a stack of gambling losses afford a place like that?" I asked. "You and I need to pay him a visit."

"Just the two of you?" said Daniel.

"Yes. You need to keep showing up for work like nothing's wrong. And keep an eye on Wardour and McCardy as best you can, without tipping them off. Sam and Eddie also have jobs they need to do, and anyway, it's outside Eddie's jurisdiction, which always makes things messy."

"How do you plan on us getting there?" asked Joy. "I can't ask Madge to lend me a cab for a trip that far."

"I have an idea about that," I said with smile. "But it's late, so it will have to wait for tomorrow."

The following afternoon, we were sat around a table with Ginnie in the Marmont's lounge. I had explained as much as I could of the proposal without straying into confidential matters.

"A road trip to Palm Springs," said Ginnie, "and a mystery, too! Of course I'm in."

"Perfect," I said. "When can we leave?"

"It's probably a three hour drive, so let's start in the morning. I'll have the concierge here book us a villa for a couple of nights. Meanwhile, we need to take you clothes shopping, Joy."

Joy looked miserable. "I hate shopping for fancy clothes almost as much as I hate wearing them. You know that."

"I know, but if you show up there in your usual outfit, you'll stick out like… like… I don't know."

"A poor person at a rich person's resort?" I offered. Similes were not really my forte.

"I promise it won't take long," said Ginnie. "We will visit one store and buy you one outfit. I guarantee it will be something you will feel comfortable in."

Joy still looked unhappy, but she nodded her assent.

We finished our drinks, and headed out front. With an almost invisible nod, Ginnie instructed the doorman to whistle up a taxi for us. Ten minutes later, we were standing in front of an unassuming storefront. The window was frosted. Painted across it were the words "Ladieswear by Michelle."

"It doesn't exactly scream 'come in'," I said.

"Michelle is not particularly interested in window-shoppers or casual walk-ins," replied Ginnie.

This was a new world to me, one where actively discouraging customers was considered an appealing feature.

"It says 'by appointment only' on the door," said Joy.

"Oh, that doesn't apply to us," said Ginnie, and rang the bell.

The door was opened by a tall, elegant woman, probably in her fifties, wearing a simple black sleeveless shift, her blonde hair in an up-do that set off her fine bone structure. The store was plainly furnished, perhaps to avoid distracting from the clothes. The designs were not over-elaborate, but the materials, cut, and finish were obviously high quality. It was the kind of understatement that Ginnie carried off so well. I noticed that the shelves and racks were sparse; there was only one of each item on display. I guessed that other sizes were kept in the back to reduce visual clutter. I approved strongly.

"Ginnie," the woman said, "how lovely to see you!"

"You too, Michelle. I'm hoping you have time to help my friend Joy here. We're going to Palm Springs tomorrow, and she has absolutely nothing to wear."

Michelle's face remained a perfectly professional mask, but I suspected she had already come to that conclusion the moment Joy had stepped inside the door.

"Of course. What sort of things are we looking for?"

Joy looked at me, I assumed for emotional support. "No fancy frocks," she said.

"I'm thinking linen pants, silk blouses, and something in case the evenings turn cold," said Ginnie.

Michelle looked Joy up and down, figuring her size with an expert eye, then moved efficiently around the store and in and out of the backroom. Thirty minutes later, the clothes were stacked on the counter. Two pairs of linen pants, one white ("for day wear", Ginnie explained) and one cream ("for evenings"). Three raw silk blouses in ivory, cream, and pearl (or "white, white, and white," as Joy described them).

And an impossibly soft and lightweight collarless leather jacket in almost the same shade of brown as Joy's flight jacket. It was as close as you could get to Joy's everyday clothes while still spending more than a hundred dollars.

"Now shoes," said Ginnie.

"No heels," stated Joy firmly.

"Of course," said Ginnie.

Michelle promptly offered up a pair of flat pumps in sunshine yellow that, to my surprise, brought a smile to Joy's face.

"I'll hem the pants this evening," said Michelle, "and you can pick everything up first thing tomorrow."

We stepped outside.

"Was that so terrible?" Ginnie teased Joy.

"Not terrible," she replied, "but I would very much like a beer now."

Chapter Seventeen

We were on the road by nine the next morning, heading east on route 60 and hoping to make it to Palm Springs by lunchtime. Once outside the city limits, the Caddie cruised effortlessly at a steady fifty-five. Joy was up front alongside Ginnie, enjoying what she had described as by far the best car she had ever ridden in. Ginnie drove a midnight blue Cadillac 62 Coupe, and she drove it with great confidence. I sat in the back, trying to come up with sort of plan once we arrived. I couldn't make up my mind whether it would be better to beard Hathaway directly, or stalk him for a while first. I had even less idea what I would say to him.

About an hour outside LA, we hit a long, straight stretch of highway with heat-shimmered desert on both sides all the way to the horizon.

"How fast can this go?" asked Joy.

"The dealer claimed one hundred. Shall we find out?" replied Ginnie.

Before I could raise my voice in dissent, Ginnie had already floored the pedal. The big V8 engine responded gleefully, like a dog that had finally been let off its leash. We passed sixty almost immediately and in what seemed like no time, passed seventy. As we approached eighty, it finally felt as though the acceleration was slowing. The needle touched ninety just as we passed a massive roadside billboard.

Almost immediately, we heard the sirens. I looked back and saw the flashing lights. We were outpacing the patrol car for the moment, but trying to outrun it seemed like a very bad idea. Ginnie obviously agreed. She slowed the car, pulled over to the shoulder, set the brake, turned off the engine, and wound down the window. My stomach was in knots, but Ginnie looked preternaturally calm.

The patrol car pulled in behind us. The officer got out, positioned his cap carefully on his head, smoothed the creases from the lap of his pants, and approached the car.

"License please, ma'am," he said.

"Of course," said Ginnie.

She handed him her license. He unfolded it, and inside was a card with writing I couldn't make out. The patrolman looked at the license then read the card. He refolded the license, handed it back to Ginnie, and gave a half-hearted salute.

"Please drive more carefully in future, ma'am," he said.

"Of course," replied Ginnie. "Thank you for your courtesy, officer."

The officer walked back to his car, stooped inside, turned it around, and headed back to his billboard.

"Now I need to know what was on the card," I said.

"Oh," said Ginnie, "it's just a personal note signed by CHP Chief Cato, thanking me for my generous contributions to the highway patrol's orphans and widows charity, and encouraging any officers who might encounter me to offer their utmost assistance."

"That's very kind of him," I said. "Now, can we stick to fifty-five from here on?"

Joy and Ginnie laughed, but I slumped back in the seat. I was torn about our encounter. On the one hand, without the note, the officer might readily have arrested

Ginnie and impounded the car, which would have been disastrous. On the other hand, I did not feel comfortable with the idea that the rich could so casually buy their way out of traffic stops. I stewed on that for much of the remainder of the journey.

We arrived at La Quinta around one o'clock. It was as impressive as I'd expected from Ginnie's description. An understated stone monument marked the entrance to a horseshoe court of low buildings of white adobe and orange tiles in the popular southwest style. Tall palms stood sentry all around. Behind, the roofs of casitas poked above the main hotel, and beyond, towered a skyline of red-brown mountains. It really did seem to be the fabled desert oasis.

Ginnie pulled into a parking slot, stepped out, and handed the keys to an eager valet who had magically appeared at carside.

"Townsend," she said.

The valet went over to the concierge stand, consulted a list, and nodded.

"Well, I for one could use a drink," she continued, heading into the lobby and turning to her left, her familiarity obvious. Joy and I scurried to keep pace.

"What about the bags?" asked Joy. "And the car?"

I had been wondering the same.

"The bags will be in our casita by the time we've had a drink," replied Ginnie, "and they'll take care of the car."

Even after knowing her for a year, I still couldn't get used to the way Ginnie casually assumed that the world around her would adjust and arrange itself to her convenience. With rare exceptions, it generally did.

We chose a table in an interior brick-laid courtyard, shaded by a large yellow umbrella. The air was dry, with the temperature comfortably in the mid-seventies. If they had climate-controlled the whole courtyard, they couldn't have arranged it better. Ginnie ordered a Tom Collins. Joy asked for a beer. I ordered coffee. I needed a pick-me-up more than a relaxant.

With drinks in hand, I turned to Ginnie.

"This is a foreign country to me," I said. "What do you suggest?"

"There is a pre-dinner cocktail reception at five," she replied. "We might be able to find your man there."

"And if we do?"

"I'll approach him and make conversation, and see what I can get out of him casually."

It made sense. Hathaway would be shocked and immediately suspicious to see me here. We had no idea what, if anything, he knew about Joy. But this was Ginnie's native habitat. She could pull off a casual encounter over cocktails far better than either one of us.

"In the meantime?" I asked.

"A leisurely drink, a rest, and a shower, I suggest."

We followed her advice.

We roused ourselves around four-thirty and dressed. Ginnie was wearing another one of her simple-yet-brilliant sleek dresses. This one was emerald green, a little lower in the neckline and shorter in the skirt than I'd seen on her before. On her feet were a pair of matching stilettos that I would never attempt.

"It's what I wear to go hunting," she said.

It took me a moment to figure that out. I was wearing a simple black cocktail dress with full-length sleeves and my favorite black pumps. Ginnie had helped me put my hair up in an arrangement that she assured me was not too formal or elaborate, but just right for evenings here.

Joy was evaluating herself in the full-length mirror, turning this way and that. She was wearing the cream pants, the ivory blouse, and the jacket. The shoes added the perfect pop of color to her subdued outfit. She had refused to let Ginnie arrange her hair.

"What do you think?" asked Ginnie.

"I have to confess," replied Joy, "I don't hate it."

"The next time you work one of my parties, you won't have to pass as a waitress," Ginnie said with a teasing smile.

"And have to make conversation with rich people? No thanks. I'd rather serve drinks and eavesdrop on them."

"Maybe you should stay back here, in case Hathaway spots you," Ginnie said to me.

"No, I'm coming," I replied. "You'll need me to point him out to you. If he spots me, we'll just have to confront him directly about what he's doing here."

We strolled over to the main building. We found the party in a small ballroom. It was not long after five and the crowd was still sparse. Waiters bearing trays of champagne cocktails circulated silently.

"Do you see him?" asked Ginnie.

I scanned the room.

"The slim blonde woman in the dark blue dress," I said. "He's with her."

"Oh, the dress is lovely. I had one just like it last season."

In Ginnie's circles, this was considered a devastating putdown. It was also literally true of half of my wardrobe.

"Okay," she said, "I have to handle the next part alone. Go to a bar and relax. If you want to eat here, use one of the cafés, not the main dining room."

Ginnie glided into the room, lifting a glass from a passing tray without breaking stride, and crossed the floor, apparently wandering at random and yet somehow quickly finding herself next to Hathaway and the blonde. Within moments, they were chatting and laughing together, Ginnie touching them both on the elbows in an assumption of intimacy that was beyond me.

"Alright," said Joy, "let's make ourselves scarce. Do you think I can order a beer in this outfit?"

"Yes," I replied, "but don't be surprised if it comes with a little umbrella and a slice of fruit."

We scouted out the location of the main dining room, and then found a café that anybody coming from the cocktail party would have to pass. We positioned ourselves where Joy could keep an eye out. I had my back to the passers-by. We drank slowly and waited. Around the room, flirting couples negotiated over love or money.

"Hey, they're coming," said Joy.

"Do they look happy together?" I asked.

"Well, she has one of them on each arm."

"How does she do it?"

"Beats me. Nothing to do now but wait," said Joy.

We drank lightly and ate sparsely, both of us too anxious to have much appetite. People with jewels and fine wristwatches came and went. Some wore expensive clothes. The others, expensive clothes wore them.

The three of them returned an hour later, Ginnie skillfully steering their path so that they were looking away from us. She appeared to be saying some sort of goodnight, exchanging air kisses with the woman before watching the two of them walk away in the direction of the casitas, arm in arm. The happy couple.

Once Ginnie was certain they were gone, she came over to our table and took a seat. A waiter magically appeared and took her order for a Rob Roy.

"Gosh, that was fun," said Ginnie.

"Okay, dish!" said Joy.

"Well. She claims to be Helene Tudor, from a well-to-do family in Dayton. Not rich, but sort of lower-upper-middle class. The youngest of three sisters. The father is a doctor."

I wondered if Ginnie always parsed social classes so finely.

"They met a couple of weeks ago at a restaurant," she continued. "They were both dining alone, so she invited him to join her, and they immediately hit it off. They've been seeing each other ever since."

"So that would be right around the time Hathaway did the thing that we can't tell you about," I said. I felt bad even as I said that out loud.

"He did say he had been eating out to celebrate some triumph at work," replied Ginnie, "but that it was awfully hush-hush and he couldn't say what. Helene didn't know either, or at least, that's what she claimed."

"What were they like together?" asked Joy.

"Like a couple that's not been together long enough to irritate each other yet, having a swell time at a fine resort. Anyway, after they'd been seeing each other for a week or so, she'd said she wanted to escape the winter, and he'd said he had some leave he could take, and here they are. It's their first time, so they were happy to meet somebody like me who knows her way around."

"That's quite the whirlwind romance," said Joy.

"Practically a fairy tale," I said. "Ginnie, I hate to do this to you, but Joy and I need to discuss next steps confidentially."

"It's alright," she said. "I rather expected that would be part of the deal. I'm going to check out the cocktail bar and see if there are any decent single men here. The pickings surely have to be better than back home. Don't wait up for me."

She drained her cocktail, picked up her clutch, and strolled off.

"All sounds a bit too good to be true, doesn't it?" said Joy.

"Absolutely," I replied. "Do you want to take first shot at it?"

"Sure. The way I see it, the Soviets decide that it would be extremely useful to have something on Hathaway. Owning him would be a huge help in protecting their operation inside the TDL, once they restart it. So they plan to have him meet an attractive, but not suspiciously beautiful, young woman who just happens to be a Soviet agent in her spare time. Now they wait for him to compromise himself by sharing something confidential. Or failing that, a photographer hides in their closet and jumps out and photographs them in a compromising position."

I wasn't entirely sure whether that last was a joke. It was a thing that did sometimes happen in the sleazier kind of divorce investigation. It was absolutely not a tactic we would use.

"Maybe they had already decided to rid themselves of Lewis," I said. "So they convert Hathaway from Lewis's unwitting dupe into an active agent on their behalf. She would be perfect as a replacement channel for money for Hathaway's poker habit. Not to mention paying for this getaway, perhaps."

"Perhaps Lewis had even figured out he was being replaced. Going AWOL to come to LA and then trying to kill one of us does seem like a desperate move. Maybe it was a last throw of the dice to try to win back his place."

"If so, it backfired horribly," I said.

"It's a neat story. It's a shame we don't have a shred of evidence. Any ideas?"

"Let's rule out breaking into their casita. If she's any good at all, she won't have brought anything incriminating with her. Too hard to hide when you're sharing a room."

"I suppose we can ask Ginnie to keep an ear open for any contradictions or holes in her story. But it's hard to ask her to do more without being able to tell her what we're looking for."

"Maybe Ginnie can get her away from Hathaway for a while," I said. "Then we can get into conversation with her, and see if she lets anything slip."

"I can't think of anything better right now," said Joy.

We got the plan rolling the next morning. Ginnie took us out for brunch.

"I think it worked," she said. "I told Hathaway how generous it was of him to bring his girlfriend out here. Then I suggested it would be nice if he bought her a little gift to remember it by, and would he like me to help him pick something out. He went for it."

"That's brilliant," said Joy.

"I'm going to meet him in the lobby at one, and will keep him busy for at least a couple of hours. You should find her by the pool."

"Perfect," I said. "Joy, you might have to carry the conversation. You know how I am with strangers."

"I've got you, kid," she said.

We found Helene laying out on a lounger, wearing Bermuda shorts, a simple tee-shirt, and a broad-brimmed hat. She had a book in her hand and a tall bright-orange drink on the table beside her. Joy took the lounger next to her, and I sat next to Joy.

"Do you mind some company?" said Joy. "It's our first time here and we know absolutely nobody."

And just like that, Joy was off and running.

"Me too," said Helene. "It's wonderfully glamorous, isn't it?"

"I know! Have you seen any Hollywood types yet?"

"Not a one, but I'm not giving up hope."

"Oh, we should introduce ourselves. I'm Joy, this is my friend Dot. We're having a little winter break without our husbands. Are you by yourself?"

"Nice to meet you," she replied. "I'm Helene. And no, I'm here with my boyfriend."

"Well, this is generous of him. He seems like a catch."

Joy was probably screaming inside when she said that. I would owe her a beer later.

"He is, but not because he's rich. Far from it. Actually, I'm not even sure how he's stretching to this."

Was it really true that he was paying? I wondered. Or was that just her sticking to her cover?

"Is he around?" asked Joy.

"Not at the moment. He had to go off and do something mysterious. He's often doing that." She paused, looked around theatrically, then lowered her voice to a whisper. "He works in military intelligence! Isn't that exciting?"

"Gosh, yes. He must have some great stories to tell."

"Oh, not at all. He doesn't talk about work ever, and told me he never will. Actually, I rather like that. Who wants to listen to men droning on about their jobs?"

"I'm with you on that," said Joy.

I realized I had said nothing, but I was struggling to come up with anything more subtle than "What are your feelings about Stalin?" That didn't seem right for this conversation.

"What about you two?" said Helene. "What do your husbands do?"

"They both do something in banking. Please don't ask me to explain it."

"Me neither," I said. Was this kind of conversation where life was going for American women now?

This was getting us nowhere. I was getting an itch to break into her casita after all, just to feel like I was doing something useful. Breaking in somewhere seemed to be my default response when I was frustrated with an investigation. *You know what,* another part of my brain said, *this is the ideal time to do it—with Hathaway out of the picture and Helene tied up with Joy.*

"Would you excuse me for a few minutes?" I said.

I walked over to reception. The girl behind the counter cheerfully told me which casita Helene and Hathaway were staying in, and even drew me a little sketch of how to get there.

I found it easily enough. The door was locked, and not the kind of lock I could pick, but the windows were single-hung with simple latches. I pulled my pocketknife from my purse, slipped it into the gap between the panes, flicked the latch open, and lifted the lower pane. I stuck my head inside and listened in case a maid was in there, but I heard nothing. I straddled the sill and dropped inside. It was far from elegant, but it worked.

The casita was basically identical in layout to ours. Two bedrooms, a shared bathroom, and a living room with a couch, a couple of rattan chairs, and a glass-topped coffee table. I had no idea whether they were sharing a bed after such short acquaintance, but decided to start with the bedroom with the two single beds. Each had a bedside table with the same lamp and ashtray as ours. The tabletops were clear, and the drawers were empty. I checked the closet. His clothes were in there, a few shirts, a couple of pairs of casual slacks that looked brand new, and in the drawers, a three or four day supply of underwear.

I went next door to the double. Here, one of the bedside tables had a few trinkets on it, some modest jewelry, and a lighter of no great value. In the drawer, a few coins. The closet contained nothing but the clothes of a woman on a brief resort break.

So far this was a complete bust.

And then I heard the lock rattle. Hathaway couldn't possibly be back so soon, could he? I looked at the closet and wondered whether somebody really could hide inside. And then I thought about how ridiculous I would look if he discovered me in there.

I would just have to face this head on.

I went out into the living room just as Hathaway came in. He was carrying a small silver shopping bag, presumably with some charming piece of jewelry inside. He stared at me for several long, silent seconds.

"What on Earth are you doing here?" he said.

"I was going to ask you the same question," I said.

"It's my room. I'm supposed to be here."

"No, I meant here at this expensive resort."

"I'm on vacation with my girlfriend, if it's any of your business. So again, why are you in my room?"

"Can we sit down?" I said with a heavy sigh. "There's something important we need to discuss."

We arranged ourselves around the small coffee table.

"You should know that Lewis has been murdered," I told him. I paused for a few moments to see how he would handle that.

"Details?" he said, impassionately.

"He followed me back to LA, where he tried to run me down. A few days later, he was found in his car with a fatal knife wound to the back of his neck."

"And are you going to tell me why, or is that too confidential for the likes of me?" he asked sardonically.

"No, you need to know. We think that Weber was set up to take the fall for the spying. We don't think he was involved at all. However, we do think Lewis was involved, possibly using Dr. Reardon."

Hathaway looked a little less blank now. "It was Lewis who tipped me off to Weber as the source of the leaks. He also encouraged me to go over to his room right away, in case there was any incriminating evidence. Take him by surprise, as it were."

"We know Lewis has other collaborators and we're trying to figure out who they are. We don't know who killed him yet, or why. It might even have been his own people."

"And what does that all have to do with me?"

"We were concerned that Lewis's associates were looking to replace him with you. So they would set you up with an attractive woman who is, in fact, their agent, who would trick you into doing something incriminating, and then blackmail you to continue working for them."

"Do you think I'm not aware of that danger in my position?"

"Just how confident are you in Helene?"

"I've been to her house. Met her parents, drank their gin. I had tea with her sisters. I think they were vetting me, actually. If it's a cover, it's the most elaborate ruse I've ever seen. What, did you think she was too attractive to be with a lump like me?"

I felt my cheeks burning. "Well… she is very pretty, isn't she? And there's also the money."

"What money?"

"I learned about your poker game. Where are you getting the money to pay for your losses?"

"I don't lose. I do quite well. I could do a lot better, but if I took them for as much as I could, they probably wouldn't let me play anymore."

"But I heard that you always lose at the game on base?"

"Yes, I do. It costs me a few pennies and a bottle of whiskey, which the other game pays for quite comfortably. It's also paying for this splurge trip, in case you were wondering."

"But why?"

"I don't think you have any idea how hard it is for an intelligence officer to have friends. Everybody thinks you're watching them all the time. So I play cards badly, loosen them up with whiskey, and lose uncomplainingly. I'm basically paying them to be my friends once a week."

"Oh," I said. "I owe you a huge apology. It seems I have completely underestimated you."

"I'll share a little secret with you. Being underestimated is a huge asset for an intelligence officer."

"You're not going to tell Helene about this are you?"

"Oh, absolutely I am. Not the part about Lewis, obviously. But she's going to get a huge kick out of being taken for a Soviet spy sent to seduce me."

"I should leave now."

"Yes. In fact, you should leave the whole resort. It's going to be very awkward if we keep bumping into each other. And by that, I mean awkward for you."

"You're right. Sorry again."

I found Joy in the lobby, and Ginnie with her.

"Oh, there you are," said Ginnie. "I've been looking all over. Hathaway bought something at the very first store we went to, and came right back."

"I ran into him," I replied.

"And?" said Joy.

"I'll tell you in the car. We need to leave. Right now."

We went to our room and packed in silence, then went back to reception. Ginnie dispatched a valet to bring her car around and another to fetch our bags.

Once the resort was finally disappearing in the desert dust kicked up by Ginnie's tires, Joy broke the silence.

"If Helene's not the genuine article," said Joy, "she is a Hollywood caliber actress."

"I know," I said morosely. I gave them the whole humiliating story.

And then I said not another word for the three hour ride home.

Chapter Eighteen

The next morning, Joy and I met with Eddie at the station. Daniel was at his office, trying to maintain a façade of normality.

"Well, that was another frustrating dead end," I said. "Did we miss anything while we were away?"

"Something big, actually. Daniel called in a favor from a friend in CIG. He dusted Daniel's safe. You'll never guess whose fingerprints they found."

"Wardour?" said Joy.

"Yep. They matched them to prints from some paperwork he'd handled."

"That was careless of him. But it seems pretty conclusive," I said.

"It gets worse," said Eddie. His face was creased with anxiety. I had never seen him get worked up over a case before, not even the grisliest murder. Was it because he still thought I was in danger?

"Yesterday, Wardour told Daniel to turn over all of his original notes as well as your final report. Daniel stalled him by saying he had to catalog everything and redact names first, but he'll have to give them up today."

"Those notes are going to mysteriously disappear, aren't they?" said Joy. "Wardour is erasing his tracks."

"I'll bet Daniel's official report vanishes too, if it hasn't already," I added. "We're not going to be able to prove anything without a paper trail."

"We have to stop him somehow," said Joy, "and we have to do it right now."

"Let's follow Wardour when he leaves the office tonight," I replied. "If there's any chance he's taking the material with him, we need to know where he goes, and if he tries to stash it or destroy it."

"Even better, if we can catch him with confidential material on him, we can nail him," said Eddie. "There's just one problem."

"What's that?" asked Joy.

"As a field agent, he'll have been trained in counter-surveillance. If OSS is as good as Daniel said, he'll know how to spot a tail, and how to shake one. If we're going to have any chance, we need a team, rotating in and out. It'll make us a whole lot harder to spot."

"The three of us, then."

"No good. He knows you, and there's a decent chance he also knows Joy. If he spots either of you, the jig is up."

"What about Sam Lowry?" Joy said. "I hate to drag anybody else into this, but if anybody can take care of themselves, it's Sam."

"Wait, you know Sam Lowry?" Eddie asked.

"Yes, we've worked with him a couple of times. And he's a good friend. You know him too?"

"Only by reputation," he replied. "He retired before I became a detective, but he's a bit of a legend in the squad room. He keeps up with some of his old buddies in Robbery, which is often useful in his line of work."

"We should ask Daniel for permission before briefing Sam," I said.

"I think we're beyond caring about formalities at this point," said Joy. "This can't wait."

I gave Sam a call to make sure he was available, and he told us to come right over. The three of us piled into Eddie's car and we made it across town in thirty minutes.

Inside, Sam was stationed on his usual spot, surveying the lobby. Standing next to him was his apprentice Frankie, alertly making sure that nobody tried to steal the chandelier, the columns, or the velvet-covered benches. As far as I could see, he was doing a great job. Frankie was a kind of stray Sam had picked up last year. He had been scammed by a company that sold him a mail-order course on becoming a private detective that turned out to be a complete dud. Sam had taken him under his wing and was teaching him to do it the right way, but he was still very wet behind the ears.

Sam waved us over. A few minutes later, we were seated around a table in the dining room, while Frankie stayed on duty in the lobby. Eddie introduced himself.

"Eddie Ramirez, Homicide. Everyone in the Robbery division still shares stories about you," he said.

"Nothing true, I hope," said Sam with a broad smile.

"Sam, we have a request for your help," I said. "But before I ask, I'm going to need to share some background with you. And once I do that, you're going to be involved in something dangerous. It has at least two, maybe three murders attached to it already. And the people we're dealing with are no mugs. They are smart and well-trained, and they're ruthless. Anybody involved in this might become their target. I can stop right there, walk away, no hard feelings.

We'll figure out another way. But if I go ahead, understand that you're crossing a line."

Sam didn't hesitate. "I'm in," he said. "It's been a few years since anybody tried to kill me, and I kind of miss it."

"Thank you," I said. It took about fifteen minutes to bring him up to speed.

"That's quite a mess," he said when we were done. "So what's your plan?"

"This guy is good," said Eddie. "The two of us need to tag-team him."

"I have a better idea. We'll have Frankie follow him too."

"I don't get it," said Joy, "Frankie's the least experienced of all of us."

"Yeah, that's the point," said Sam grinning. "Wardour will make Frankie, and once he shakes him, he'll be less likely to be looking for the real tails. After Frankie loses Wardour, he can go back to the hotel where he'll be well away from any trouble when we take Wardour. We can all take care of ourselves, but Frankie is just a kid."

"I like that," said Joy. "I was worried for a minute there that we'd be putting Frankie up front in something dangerous."

"I hate sitting this out," I said.

"I have an idea about that," said Joy. "Maybe we can hang around in a cab, sometimes ahead of Wardour, sometimes behind, sometimes nowhere in sight. Nobody looks at cab drivers, and I still have that blonde wig for you if you want it. If he jumps in a car, we could tail him. I haven't done that in a long while."

Eddie and Sam looked at each other.

"What do you think?" said Eddie. "This is much more in your territory than mine."

"Yeah, I guess there's not much call for tailing corpses," said Sam, with a smirk. "I think it could work, but Joy, no curb-crawling, or he'll make you straight off. You have to keep with the traffic flow, even if that means you lose him for a bit and have to double back. Or lose him completely. That's okay, because remember, you're the third line of defense here."

"Yeah, I can live with that," said Joy.

"What do we tell Frankie?" said Eddie.

"As little as possible," said Sam. "It's safer for him that way. I'll take care of it. I'll tell him it's about a guy who skipped out on his bill or something like that. I'll make sure he knows to keep his distance, too. So when do we do this?"

"It has to be this evening," I said. "If Wardour gets away with Daniel's notes today, they're gone for good. We should call Daniel to see if he knows anything about Wardour's routine."

Sam led me to his office, which looked suspiciously like a converted closet. A bare lightbulb hung from the ceiling. Banker's boxes lined the walls, stacked three deep. Underneath a blanket of papers there was, presumably, a desk. The room was barely big enough for the desk and a man of Sam's size, so he waited outside while I made the call. Daniel said nothing about my breach of protocol in briefing Sam, which I took to mean that he also understood the urgency of not letting those papers get away.

We were all in place by five twenty. Daniel had said that Wardour usually left the office at five thirty, sometimes a few minutes later, never earlier. Twice they had left the building together, and both times, Wardour had turned left in front of the building and headed south down Los Angeles Street and across Temple Street.

Conveniently, that would take him past Eddie's building. Frankie had stationed himself a half block north of the Federal Building, from where he would pick up Wardour. Eddie was waiting in the lobby of the police station and would fall in behind Frankie as he passed. Sam was across the street and would follow on that side. If Wardour crossed Los Angeles Street at any point, he and Eddie would switch roles.

Joy and I would circle the block in a cab and try to pick Wardour up as best we could. If it looked at any point like Wardour was ditching the materials, Sam and Eddie would move in. And Daniel would stay in the office as our controller, in case anybody needed to call in. We figured the plan was about as solid as we could make it under the circumstances, although everybody was still anxious.

Wardour emerged a couple of minutes after five thirty. He looked left and right, then turned left, just as we had hoped. Frankie loped off after him. Joy rounded the corner from Aliso Street and passed Wardour before he reached Temple Street, and then cruised on down to First Street, made a right, and circled the block back to Los Angeles Street. We didn't see him, but then I spotted Eddie crossing over and heading up First Street. Wardour was heading towards the park in front of City Hall.

We passed him again just after Main Street and saw him turn into a bodega. Frankie stopped half a block back, and looking behind, I could see Sam and Eddie another half block behind, one on each side of First Street. Joy carried on past the park, made a right and circled City Hall.

We caught up to him again a couple of blocks further up. He was carrying a brown paper grocery bag. He turned left on Broadway.

"I hope he hasn't made us already," Joy said. "Making a left at a busy intersection is a good way for a pedestrian to lose a tail in a car. On the other hand, cutting through the park would have been even more effective, so maybe not."

Nonetheless, we continued our dance, passing him and circling the block. At this time of day, there were plenty of taxis, so it would be remarkable if he had picked us out.

The next time we saw him, he was sitting outside a café, his grocery bag on the chair next to him. Frankie had taken a table as far away as possible and behind him, but that still gave him a line of sight. I didn't see Sam or Eddie, but assumed they were close by. Joy pulled the cab over half a block down the street. We waited. A waiter came over and took Wardour's order. We waited some more. The waiter came back with a coffee.

"This tail job is turning into a stakeout," muttered Joy impatiently.

And then it all went to pieces.

A waiter emerged from the café, a trayful of wine and beer glasses on his upturned hand. As he approached Wardour's table, Wardour stood up and blocked the waiter. We couldn't hear from where we were parked, but it looked like he was shouting at the waiter and poking him in the chest. Then he shoved the waiter hard, sending the glasses tumbling, splashing beer and wine over nearby customers. The waiter let his tray fall and grabbed Wardour by the front of his shirt, pushing him back into his table. He swung a fist and connected. Two more waiters ran over, and restrained the first before he could land another punch on Wardour. They dragged him back a couple of steps. Wardour straightened up, tucked his shirt in, dropped a bill on the table, and walked away.

I looked over to see if Frankie was still on him. His table was empty. I looked back for Wardour. He had vanished. Eddie and Sam were sprinting to Frankie's now-vacant table. We jumped out of the cab, slamming the doors behind us, and ran to join them.

"Dammit," said Sam. "They've snatched him."

"We were set up," said Eddie. "Wardour provoked the fight deliberately to distract us."

I stared at the ground. "This is my fault. This was my idea."

"It's nobody's fault," said Sam. "Or everybody's. None of us knew he had a partner. And none of us expected anything like this."

"We can beat ourselves up about it later. What we need to do now," said Eddie, "is regroup and figure out our next step."

"Jack's?" said Joy.

Eddie shook his head. "We need clear heads for this."

"Our office," said Joy.

We piled into the cab, and fifteen minutes later, we were sat around my desk, four cups of mediocre coffee in front of us. The mood was solemn.

"They must have had the whole routine figured out well in advance," said Sam. "I'm guessing it's usually used to lose a tail, not kidnap one. You run it the other way around with your partner creating the disturbance, and while the tail is distracted, you disappear."

Daniel joined us in the office. I'd phoned him when we'd got here, and he'd come directly over. We quickly brought him up to date.

"I hope it wasn't the cab that gave us away," said Joy. She looked completely miserable.

"It could have been any of us," said Sam. "I think the guy is just that good."

"No, it must have been us," I said. "If he'd spotted you or Eddie, he would have just shaken you and got on with his business. He has no idea who you are. But when he sees us, he realizes we're onto him. That's when he decided he needed a bargaining chip."

"Unless he immediately came up with the plan to take Frankie as soon as he clocked him, just to find out who he was," said Sam. "We really don't know, and speculating will get us nowhere."

"But what does he want with Frankie?" said Joy. "This seems like a desperation move."

"I have no idea," said Daniel. "I can't imagine what his endgame can be."

"I'm hoping they just took Frankie for leverage," said Sam, "but I don't know what exactly. I hope the kid's okay. I should never have put him in danger like this." Sam shook his head.

"So what now? Eddie, can you get an arrest warrant for him?" Joy said.

"No chance," said Eddie. "Everything we have is circumstantial. If I brought what we have to the DA, he'd laugh me out of his office."

"You're right," I said. "The guy is absolutely dirty, but what can we definitively prove? We can't even tie him to Frankie's kidnapping. He could plausibly deny he'd ever seen Frankie and was no more involved than anybody else in the café. And by now, the incriminating paperwork is probably in ashes."

"So what now?" said Joy.

"We sit tight and wait for their next move. If Sam is right about why they took Frankie, then eventually, they have to contact us."

"And if he's wrong?"

"Let's not talk about that."

We didn't have to wait long. My phone rang. I picked up. It was Wardour.

"Listen very carefully to my instructions," he said. He spoke steadily and clearly. I took it all down in shorthand. After he hung up, I read it out to the others:

I will exchange the boy for Morgan. The exchange will take place at Forest Lawn Memorial Park at 10pm tonight. You will bring Morgan to the park. Drive yourself. Do not come in a taxi. You will park near the entrance on Glendale Avenue. The gates will be closed. I am sure you can solve that problem. You will walk together to the Great Mausoleum, stopping twenty feet from me. Morgan will then walk towards me. Once I have him secured, I will release the boy. He will then walk to you without looking back. You and the boy will leave immediately, returning the way you came.

If you fail to show up, I will kill the boy.

If anybody else is with you, I will kill the boy.

If I have reason to think anybody is watching us, I will kill the boy.

If the boy looks back, I will kill Morgan.

If you attempt to follow me, I will kill Morgan.

If your friends attempt to rescue him, I will kill Morgan.

"It's very thorough, isn't it?" said Joy.

"I almost admire it, in a strange way," I replied. "I wish all threats were so clear."

"It's a good plan," said Sam. "Well thought out. Inaccessible location late at night, so there'll be no passers-by to worry about. Cars can't approach closely, so no cavalry to the rescue. Once the handoff is done, you're fifteen minutes from your car, if you even thought about following him. And he can disappear into the darkness while you're walking. It's exactly how I'd do it."

"So what do we do now?" I asked.

"Exactly what the note says," said Daniel. "Anything else is likely to end very badly. We've all seen how good these people are. And how dangerous."

"Plus, we have no idea how many people he will have in support," said Eddie. "Sam, Joy, we agree? No attempted heroics?"

"Yes," said Sam. "We've put Frankie in enough danger already."

"We play this absolutely straight," said Joy.

"Daniel, are you sure about this?" I asked. I looked over at him. He was very pale.

"Yes," he said, a little tremor in his voice. "The boy's in danger. I have to do this."

"Okay, there's a couple of practical problems we need to talk about," I said. "One, the gates are going to be locked. They're not the kind of thing I can pick. And the fence is about ten feet high with iron spikes on the top."

"I think I can sort that out," said Eddie. "I can try to arrange for somebody to open the gate. I'll tell them it's a confidential police operation." He went over to Joy's desk and started dialing.

"Okay, thanks. Number two, I'm going to need a car. The note said no taxi, but I don't know why."

"A taxi is another possible source of a leak," said Daniel. "Suppose the taxi driver starts telling his friends about the strange late night job he had. They don't want that kind of gossip circulating."

"I have an idea how I can wrangle something," said Sam. "Joy, how long will it take to drive there from the Belvedere?"

"At that time of night, I'd say thirty minutes," said Joy.

"Okay, all of you meet me outside there at nine o'clock. That should give you some margin for traffic and still leave plenty of time to walk from the gate to the Mausoleum."

"Thanks. I'll try to take good care of your car," I said. "But I should warn you, I don't drive very often."

"Out of curiosity, when was the last time?" asked Sam.

"About a year ago."

"How'd it go?"

"I stole a car to escape a kidnapping of my own, drove pell-mell down a winding canyon road, and wrecked it at the bottom just before the PCH."

Sam, Eddie, and Daniel all stared at me.

"I'll tell you about it some other time," I added. "It's a good story."

Sam headed back to the hotel to arrange my ride. The rest of us went over to Jack's, promising ourselves just one drink, because we needed clear heads, before switching to water. Every time the minute hand of the clock ticked forward, it tightened the knot in my stomach by one more twist. I didn't know if it was literally possible to die from anxiety, but I didn't want to find out. Despite what the others had said about shared responsibility, this was on me. If anything went wrong, I would have to carry that guilt.

Around eight, we stepped out to get something to eat at a local diner. My stomach couldn't handle much, so it ended up being the most expensive bread roll I had ever bought. From there we headed over to the Belvedere. We arrived a few minutes before nine. Sam was standing outside. Next to him was a 1939 black Ford V8. It was about as unremarkable and generic a car as you could hope to find.

"How did you get hold of this?" Joy asked.

"It belongs to one of our guests," replied Eddie. "I had one of the car-hops pull it around from the garage, then told him to amscray."

"It's kind of him to let us borrow it," I said.

Eddie paused. "I didn't exactly ask permission. But provided it's back by the morning, undamaged, he'll never know."

"Feeling alright?" I said to Daniel.

"Absolutely," he replied.

I didn't believe him. I felt scared, and I wasn't even the one giving myself up. He must have been absolutely terrified. If so, he was doing an amazing job of hiding it.

I slipped behind the wheel and wound down the window, and Daniel sat himself on the other side.

"Be careful," Joy told me, "and stay safe."

I pushed the starter and the engine puttered into life. I crunched the gears getting into first. Eddie winced, and Joy shuddered.

"When this is all over," she said, "we're going to give you some driving lessons."

I eased the car away from the curb and pointed the car towards Beverly Hills. We drove in silence for forty minutes and pulled up near the entrance as instructed. As Eddie had promised, the pedestrian gate was unlocked. We passed through.

We walked side by side along the path. The rising Moon was about three-quarter full and threw just enough light for us to be able to see our way. As we approached the Mausoleum, I didn't see anybody waiting. We stopped on the path anyway, twenty feet from the building. I checked my watch. We were five minutes early. I hoped that wasn't going to mess everything up.

Suddenly, a light blinded me, and I put my hand up to cover my eyes. It flicked over to Daniel and he did the same.

I had completely lost my night vision. I wondered if that was intentional. If so, it was a clever move. I could see the beam of the flashlight now, but nothing behind it. The kidnapper and, I hoped, Frankie were completely hidden in the impenetrable shadow of the Mausoleum.

"Show me Frankie is unharmed," I called out.

Silence.

"Proof of life, or no exchange," I said.

More silence. Then a tall, skinny, hooded figure with his hands tied together that I could only assume was Frankie stepped out of the shadow and into the wan moonlight.

"Now they both walk. I know you have a gun, so you know there'll be no funny business."

Another long silence. Finally, an arm reached out and removed Frankie's hood. It gave him a shove in the back. He began to walk towards me. I nudged Daniel and he started walking slowly but steadily towards the flashlight. He stepped into the shadow and disappeared so completely, he might as well have fallen down a well. I wondered whether he would ever climb out.

Frankie reached me and paused, still facing away from the kidnapper. I turned too, and led him back down the hill and towards the car. We passed out through the gate where we paused for me to untie Frankie. It had gone perfectly, apart from the fact that I had just handed over Daniel to a ruthless murderer.

I led Frankie back to the car. Finally, I felt safe to speak. "How are you?" I asked.

"I'm okay," he said.

"Great. We're going to see Sam and Joy, and then we'll debrief."

"Okey-doke. I'll save it for when we're all there."

He really did seem unfazed. I was astonished and impressed in equal measure.

We arrived back at the Belvedere just before eleven, and found Sam, Joy and Eddie in the bar. Sam asked for a pint of beer and handed it off to Frankie, who supped gratefully. The barman looked to be about to ask for Frankie's ID, but Sam gave him a glare that even I could decode. He went back to polishing glasses.

We settled around a table. Sam took the lead. "First off, Frankie, we all owe you an apology," he said. "We badly underestimated how dangerous this would get. Anyway, I hope this doesn't put you off the whole P.I. business."

"Are you kidding?" said Frankie. "This was the most exciting thing that has ever happened to me!"

We exchanged looks around the table. Nobody had expected that.

"Did they treat you badly?" asked Joy.

"Not really, no. They tied me to a chair and asked me a bunch of questions about you guys, and somebody called Morgan. I told them what I knew because it didn't seem to be secret. At first, they didn't believe I didn't know anybody called Morgan, and they shouted at me for a bit, and they threatened to cut off bits of me, which was quite scary, but after a while, they gave up on that. Then they asked me about the plan, and I told them I didn't know about a plan and that I was just told to follow a guy."

"How many of them were there?" asked Eddie.

"I only heard two voices, a man and a woman. If there was anybody else there, I didn't hear them moving or breathing. It was the woman who brought me to the cemetery, by the way."

"You heard them?" asked Eddie.

"Oh, I didn't mention that. When she kidnapped me, she put a bag over my head before she put me in the trunk, and they kept it on me the whole time."

"Did you get a look at her?" asked Sam.

"Sorry, no," replied Frankie. "She put a knife to my neck and told me not to turn around. I figured it was best to do as I was told."

"I know who the woman is," I said.

"Who?" said Sam. "And also, how?"

"The kidnapper didn't bother to blindfold Daniel before he got the chance to see her. Logically, that means she expects she is going to be recognized by her voice anyway. It has to be Mary McCardy."

"That's not good," said Eddie. "Kidnappers don't usually leave victims alive if they can identify them."

"Would somebody mind telling me who Daniel is?" said Frankie. "And actually, what the heck is going on?"

I explained the story as concisely as I could manage while Sam fetched Frankie another beer.

"Gosh," he said, when I concluded. "Just gosh."

"We didn't want to tell you all the details because we thought it would keep you safer," said Sam.

"It almost didn't, but then in the end, it did," he replied.

"You're going to have to explain that one."

"Well, after they had questioned me for a bit, I think they realized that I really didn't know anything. And then the guy said, 'The kid's just a stooge, we should kill him,' which was very scary, I don't mind admitting. And also a bit rude.

"But then the woman said 'No, I have an idea how he could be useful'. For what it's worth, I think she's the brains of the outfit. Anyway, they walked away where I couldn't hear what they were saying. After a while they came back, led me to the car, and she took me to the cemetery."

"Do you have any idea where you were?" asked Eddie.

"It was a big building, for sure," replied Frankie. "When we first got inside, the floor was hard and I could hear everybody's footsteps echoing. It was a long echo time, like a hangar."

"The air terminal, maybe?"

"I don't think so. I didn't hear any planes on the way in. And after we'd walked a bit, the floor changed. It became soft, kind of cushiony. And completely silent."

"That's some impressive recall," said Sam. "Good job!"

Frankie beamed at the compliment.

"Maybe it was a carpeted office inside a big warehouse," said Eddie. "Is there anything else you remember? Anything at all?"

"That's everything I can think of about the building. I do know how far away it is, though. Would that help?"

I was stunned. I looked around the table, and everybody was staring at Frankie.

"Um… how?" said Joy.

"The drive to the cemetery took thirty four minutes."

"How could you possibly know that?"

"I counted my heartbeats. I know what my pulse rate is, so it was easy enough to convert it to minutes and seconds."

"That's amazing. Did you come up with that yourself?"

"Please don't laugh. I heard a detective do it on a radio show. But I figured, even if it wasn't useful in real life, it might help me stay calm. I thought she was taking me somewhere to kill me."

"I don't suppose you counted when they snatched you, did you?"

"I did. Twenty six minutes."

Eddie stood up.

"Where are you going?" I asked.

"To get a streetmap from my car," he replied. "I'll be right back."

While Eddie was gone, Joy and I fetched another round of drinks for everybody except Frankie, who seemed to be doing fine with his second beer.

Eddie returned and unfolded the map on the table. We scrambled to move our drinks out of the way.

"Okay, Joy," said Eddie, "can you sketch how far thirty-four minutes from Forest Lawn would get you after nine at night? Just west and southwest for now."

"Sure, but it's going to be pretty approximate," she replied. "It's not like you can drive in a straight line anywhere in this city."

Joy rough-handed an arc that went from Beverly Hills through Culver City and then east to South LA.

"Good. Now do twenty-six minutes from the café on Broadway where Frankie was snatched."

"Okay, that was towards the end of rush hour, so…"

"Actually, no," said Frankie. "After she put me in the trunk, we didn't go anywhere for a very long time. I wasn't counting at that point, so I don't know how long."

"When you moved, did it feel like stop-go traffic?"

"No, it was mostly smooth. There were some stops, I guess for traffic lights, but when we moved, from the sounds of it, we were going a decent speed."

I looked at Frankie with admiration. His attention to detail under such stressful circumstances was truly remarkable. I was starting to think he had the makings of a fine detective. And credit to Sam, too, for what he was teaching him.

"Alright, so they waited until after rush hour, maybe even after dark," said Joy. "They might even have waited until after dark to move you to the warehouse." She roughed out another arc, crossing the first.

"Great," said Eddie. "Now, what's near the intersection of those two lines?"

We were all silent for half a minute.

"Century City," I blurted out. "I know where they are."

Everybody looked at me.

"They're holed up on a sound stage at a movie studio," I said. "Twentieth Century and Mammoth are right there."

"Makes sense," said Sam. "No sound gets in or out, so you can do whatever you want there. Even shoot somebody if you feel like it. And as long as the red light is flashing over the door, nobody is going to come in."

"Now we just need to figure out which one," said Joy.

I sighed. "We could search all night in the dark. There must be dozens of sound stages."

"I have an idea about that," replied Eddie, "but it will have to wait for the morning."

I didn't feel happy about that, and I assumed nobody else did either, but there didn't seem to be a good alternative. It was going to be a restless night for all of us.

I turned to Frankie. "Frankie, you've been brilliant," I said.

He blushed adorably.

Chapter Nineteen

We met first thing the following morning at the police station. Myself, Joy, Sam, and Frankie gathered around a conference table where Eddie has asked us to wait for him. For fifteen minutes, we sat fidgeting and drinking weak, bitter coffee before Eddie showed. He had a couple of sheets of paper in hand. We all looked at him expectantly.

"I was thinking last night, how do you set yourself up in a soundstage and nobody on the lot notices?" he said. "And I thought, if it were me, I'd set up a fake production, put the name on the outside of a soundstage, and move in."

"How do you set up a fake production?" I asked.

"I haven't figured that out yet. Work with me for the moment, though. So I called got the production schedules from both Mammoth and Twentieth Century telexed over. They list all the productions currently on their lots, when they started, when they are scheduled to end, and what sound stage they are allocated. It's how they manage sound stage availability, among other things."

"So what do we do with them?"

"We look for something anomalous. Something that suggests it's not a genuine movie production. I have no idea what that looks like, I just hope something jumps out. Read it and pass it around."

He handed one sheet to me and the other to Joy. I read it, passed it on, and waited for the other sheet to come around to me. Twentieth Century had a dozen films currently shooting, and Mammoth had half of that. Nothing struck me as strange. Not that I knew what I was looking for. I looked around the room. Everybody else looked as lost as I felt.

"Sorry, Eddie," I said. "This was a good idea, but I don't think it's going to work."

"Not so fast," said Joy. "Before we give up, let's get Ginnie down here. I bet she knows more about movies than everybody in this room together."

"Great idea," I said. "She might spot something we're all missing."

Joy made the call, and got lucky. Ginnie was taking breakfast at the Marmont, and a page found her in the lounge. She said she could be with us in thirty minutes.

She arrived as promised. She was wearing an elegantly cut dark blue skirt with a matching bolero jacket over a cream blouse with a crimson and gold scarf around her neck. She didn't simply own beautiful clothes, she knew how to wear them, and that was what made her the best-dressed person I knew. She looked amazing, and I told her so.

"So is this for the mysterious case you can't tell me about?" she asked.

"Yes, it is," I replied, "and we still can't tell you much, I'm afraid. But we do need your insight. Eddie, it was your idea. Do you want to explain?"

"Sure," he said. He handed the production lists to Ginnie. "These are all the movies currently in production at Mammoth and Twentieth Century. Anything stand out to you?"

She read through the Twentieth Century list and put it back on the table. But the Mammoth list brought her up short.

"What's this movie, *Berlin Skies*?" she asked.

Joy shrugged. "Doesn't mean anything to me."

"Me neither, and that's odd. All these others, I've read about them in the newspapers and the movie magazines. Normally, there's lots of publicity about upcoming movies while they are shooting. Sometimes even before. Who's starring, who's producing, and so on. Usually there are juicy stories that come out of the production, especially in the gossip sheets. But I've heard absolutely nothing about *Berlin Skies*."

Joy grinned. "Thanks, that's exactly what we needed."

"You're welcome. I just hope that at some point you can tell me what this is all about."

I smiled at Ginnie gratefully. She was always willing to drop everything to jump in, even when it was risky. And looking around the room, that seemed to be the case for everybody else too. Joy, Eddie, Sam, Frankie… they were all volunteering to walk into unknown danger just because I needed them to, in order to save a man they barely knew. I had been so self-reliant for so much of my life, I was astonished to feel like I was finding my place in a team. *More than that,* I mused: *Am I finding a family?*

While Ginnie headed back to her breakfast, we tried to figure out a rescue plan.

"We can't just go charging in there," said Eddie. "Those soundstages have four, maybe six doors. And there are also big doors at one end for bringing in large pieces of scenery."

"They're called elephant doors," I said.

"Right. Anyway, if we all march in together, there's a good chance they'll just kill Daniel and escape out the back. We need them to stay calm until we get close enough that they know they have no play and no way out."

I stared into the distance, letting my brain work its magic. I don't know how long I was out of it, but when I returned my attention to the room, everybody was looking at me.

"Got anything?" asked Joy.

"I have an idea, but you're probably going to hate it."

I laid out my plan.

"You're right," said Joy. "I hate it. But I can't honestly say it's the craziest idea you've ever had. Actually, it's not even the craziest idea you've had in the past week."

"Does anybody have anything better?"

Silence.

"Okay then. I can get us on the lot through the side door." I'd broken into Mammoth before, and unless they had significantly improved their security, I was confident I could do it again.

"I can get us through the front door," said Eddie. "There aren't many places a homicide detective gets turned away from."

We hustled down to the garage and piled into Eddie's cruiser, Sam up front and the rest of us squeezed in the back.

"This is neat," said Frankie. "I've never been in a police car before!"

We found a parking spot across the street from Mammoth's gate, and we followed Eddie over to the booth. Two guards were standing outside, shooing sightseers away.

They were dressed in uniforms that looked like leftovers from a cop movie and had badges pinned to their chests that looked equally fake. Eddie showed them what a real badge looked like. The rest of us flashed our P.I. buzzers.

"I'm looking for a murder suspect. I believe he's on the lot somewhere."

The two guards looked at each other, uncertain.

"I don't know, shouldn't you have a warrant?" one of them said.

"Sure, I could go get a warrant, while the murderer gets away. And then I could hold a big press conference right in front of the gates here explaining how Mammoth helped him escape. Or we could do this the quiet way. What do you think, boys?"

The guards exchanged looks again, then waved us through.

It didn't take long to find *Berlin Skies*. The soundstages all looked alike, big blocky white-stuccoed buildings with tin roofs. Fortunately, they all had the name of the assigned production on a large board outside. We took a quick reconnaissance tour around the outside. It was square, about seventy-five feet long and wide, with two doors on each of the left, right, and front walls, all locked. In back were the massive elephant doors. I pulled out my lock picks and unlocked the three doors we planned to use.

We huddled and finalized details.

"Sam and Joy, you'll come in quietly through the side doors towards the back, one on each side. Have your guns drawn and ready. I'll go in the front and hold their attention, so you can slip in behind. Eddie, take a position at the back in case they run that way. We can't open the elephant doors without making noise, so you'll have to wait outside. Frankie, you're out front."

"I'm not coming inside with you?" asked Frankie.

"No," I replied. "If everything goes wrong in there, you need to fetch help."

I gave the others a minute to get into position, then eased open the front door. This end of the building was dark, and I knew I would be silhouetted against the daylight. If they felt like shooting me, now would be the ideal moment. Cameras, boom mikes on stands, and other equipment I didn't recognize stood around on the floor. At the far end, the stage was brightly lit by a couple of overhead stage lamps. I saw three figures, a man and a woman standing, and another man seated. The lighting threw elongated shadows across the stage and onto the floor. The standing figures must be Wardour and McCardy, I thought, and Daniel was in the chair. I paused.

"Hey," shouted a male voice. Wardour. "Red light's on! Get out!"

"It's Dot Stone," I shouted back "I'm here to negotiate."

Wardour and McCardy put their heads close together for a brief conversation, then Wardour spoke again. "Close the door. Put your hands over your head and walk slowly over here."

I did as I was instructed. When I was about fifteen feet away, he told me to stop. I could see the revolver in his hand.

"It was quite clever of you to find this place," said McCardy. "I'm almost impressed." Her voice was unexpectedly silky, it made me think of a nightclub singer in a slinky dress.

"Look, it's over," I said. "Nobody else has to die. If you release Daniel alive, we can figure something out."

"What a sweet idea. But we need Daniel, I'm afraid."

"For what?"

"He's going to sign a note confessing to being a Soviet agent and to deliberately sabotaging the investigation at Wright Field, and then he's going to commit suicide. At least that was the original plan. Now he's also going to confess to killing you, before taking his own life in a fit of remorse and guilt."

"And then what? You two go back to your jobs as if nothing happened?"

"No, I think you and your friends have made things too messy for us. We will disappear."

"You mean defect?"

"If you like," said McCardy with a shrug.

"At the risk of sounding like a cliché, you won't get away with it."

"Yes, I will. And you know why? Because I'm the smartest person in the room. Practically any room, actually."

"Not quite smart enough, though. Joy, Sam, if you don't mind…"

They stepped out of the shadows behind Wardour and McCardy, their guns leveled.

"Think very carefully about your next choice," said Sam.

McCardy turned to face them. Wardour glanced over his shoulder, and kept his gun on me.

"Put the safety on the gun, and lay it on the ground," said Joy.

"Or what? You'll shoot him?" said McCardy, her voice theatrically heavy with sarcasm. "It's a lot harder to shoot a person than you might think."

"That's funny," replied Joy. "That's exactly what the last person I pointed my gun at said. Right before I shot her." She pulled back the hammer.

Wardour glanced quickly over at McCardy. Judging by the sweat beading on his brow, he was not as confident that Joy wouldn't shoot as McCardy was. Mind you, she wasn't the one Joy was pointing her gun at. He seemed jittery. Was his hand shaking? Was his nerve gone? Was this why he couldn't work in the field any longer?

"I'll shoot Stone!" he said, his voice tremulous. "I mean it!"

"Let's find out," said Joy. "Touch your trigger and see what happens."

We held precisely in that tableau for several long seconds. He started to move his finger, trembling, towards the trigger. The sound of a single gunshot exploded, followed almost immediately by a second. In that same instant, I threw myself to the ground. The sounds of the shots reverberated from the roof and hard floor, slowly dying out. I looked up. Wardour was still standing, gun in hand. A thick, dark line of blood was slowly trickling from his left ear, down his neck, towards his collar. He was making an impressive effort to look at his own ear.

"Nice shot," said Sam.

"Not really," said Joy. "I was aiming for his head. Should I try again?"

Wardour raised his left hand above his head, and with his right lowered his gun to the floor.

"Kick it away," said Sam.

He did as he was told.

"Now both of you face away from me, and put your hands behind your backs with your wrists crossed."

They did so.

"Joy, keep the woman covered," he said.

Sam approached Wardour cautiously. He gripped both of his wrists in one of his huge hands. He slipped his gun back into his shoulder holster and pulled a pair of handcuffs from his jacket pocket. Suddenly, Wardour twisted free from his grip and spun around. Out of nowhere, there was a knife was in his hand. It was a sleight of hand so fast it might have been a conjuring trick. In the same swift movement, he lunged for Sam's stomach. The broad blade sank in by an inch or more. Joy and I both ran towards him.

Sam looked down, looked back up at Wardour, and slapped him on the ear with one of his massive mitts. Wardour staggered sideways and fell to his knees. Sam pushed him down to the floor, rolled him onto his stomach, put his knee in Wardour's back, and leant his considerable weight on him. Wardour expelled his breath like a slowly-leaking balloon.

"Let's try that again," said Sam. "Hands behind your back."

"Dammit!" I heard Joy say. I looked around. McCardy had disappeared.

"We'll go after her," I said, "but first, let's get Sam some help."

Sam stood up, grinning incongruously. The knife was still embedded in his stomach, but astonishingly, there was no blood. I couldn't begin to understand how he was so calm.

"How come you're not… you know… everything?" said Joy.

Sam looked simultaneously terrifying and absurd with several inches of the knife blade protruding from his abdomen.

"You absolutely have to swear not to tell Eddie," he said. "If the boys in the squadroom hear about this…"

"Hear about what?"

"I'm wearing a corset, okay? The metal stays took most of the force out of the thrust so it only went in a little ways. And okay, yes, I might also be carrying a little extra weight around the middle, so that probably helped too."

"A corset? I never had you pegged for the vain type," said Joy.

"It's for my back pain," said Sam.

"Of course it is," smirked Joy. "We won't tell."

"Should I try to pull it out?" I asked.

"No," said Sam. "Leave it until the medics get here. As soon as you pull it out, it will bleed heavily. For now, the corset is compressing the wound, which should help."

Apparently, Sam had some experience with knife wounds. I suddenly remembered that Daniel was still gagged and tied to the chair. He had been watching the drama unfold patiently.

"Let's cut Daniel loose and round up the others," I said. "We need to get you to a doctor. At the very least, you're going to need stitches. Can you walk?"

"I think so."

A little blood was starting to seep out around the blade now, spreading slowly as it stained his shirt.

Between us, Joy and I hauled Wardour to his feet. We picked up Eddie and Frankie outside. Both of them stared at Sam, not quite able to believe how preternaturally relaxed he seemed to be. It was as if he was watching it happen to somebody else. Was this what shock looked like? Or just thirty years of experience?

"Frankie, you take care of Sam," I said. "Go with him to the hospital and make sure he gets fixed up properly. Otherwise, he's likely to say he just needs a couple of drinks and he'll walk it off."

"I'll call for a patrol car to take this one in," said Eddie. "And an ambulance for Sam. But what are we going to do about McCardy?"

"We have to go after her," I said. "If we lose her now, she'll be a ghost."

"Alright, but don't do anything until I get back with some uniforms. We need numbers to chase her down. And we need a plan. There are a thousand places she could hide here."

We watched Eddie, Sam, and Frankie until they disappeared around the corner.

Joy turned to me, head cocked to the side. "You're not going to wait, are you?" she sighed.

"We don't have time. And I think I know where she's heading. The side gate. I can get there first if she's being cautious and trying to avoid being seen."

"Let's go," said Joy. "And don't waste time telling me it's dangerous."

We set off at a fast trot. I was grateful I was wearing a pair of flats that were not impossible to run in. We rounded one last building corner and the gate came into sight.

The gate stood open.

"Damn, she got here first," I said.

"Now what?" asked Joy.

"We find the others, and figure out a plan."

As we walked back, I went over the events at the soundstage in my mind.

"I have to ask you something," I said. "Would you really have killed Wardour?"

"To keep him from hurting you, absolutely," replied Joy.

For once, I was sure she wasn't joking.

Daniel, Eddie, Joy, and I reconvened at the station. Wardour was locked in a holding cell in the basement.

"I hate to see McCardy get away," I said. "She must be long gone by now."

"Maybe not," said Daniel. "She will know there will be a dragnet out for her, so she might have gone to ground."

"I've alerted CHP, as well as the local PDs," said Eddie. "We're also sending people to watch the Soviet vice-consulate over on Glendower. If she makes it inside there, we've lost her."

"I've let the FBI know," said Daniel. "I hate to involve them, but we need their resources to watch the air terminal and the ports."

"So what now?" Joy asked. "Do we wait her out and hope to catch her if she makes a run for it?"

"I don't think we can," said Eddie. "We can't keep people on stakeout forever, just in the hope she shows up. The FBI won't, either, not for more than a couple of days. After that, her picture goes onto a Most Wanted poster and they move on to other cases."

"Then we need to set a trap to flush her out right now," I said. "And I'm the bait. She sees me as the one who ruined everything for her, and she'll want payback."

"I'm going to assume there's no point in me saying it's too dangerous and trying to talk you out of it," said Eddie with resignation.

"What if she figures it's a trap?" asked Joy.

"Oh, I'm counting on it. There's no doubt she's very smart, but she's also vain about it. If I put myself in her shoes, I would want to prove I could outsmart the trap."

"You have to make it convincing, then," said Eddie. "This only works if she believes it's a good trap, but still, she's one step ahead of you."

Joy was smirking.

"What's funny?" I asked.

"You and McCardy," she replied. "You've got a real Holmes and Moriarty thing going on here."

I scowled at her, briefly. Joy was a huge fan of Sherlock Holmes; I was not. And she always knew she could tease me by comparing me to Holmes.

"Okay, let's put our heads together," I said. "Ideas?"

"First of all," said Eddie, "it has to be something that doesn't put the general public in danger. So nowhere crowded, nowhere public. Nowhere she can grab a hostage."

"Understood," I replied.

"It also can't be a space like a park," said Daniel. "Too many places for people to hide and ambush her. She won't bite on that."

"And it can't be somewhere with just one way in and out," I said. "She has to believe she has an escape route. Ideally, a route she believes we didn't think of."

"I have an idea, but we'll need Ginnie's help again," I said. "Eddie, how many policewomen do you think the LAPD could gather for an evening of free entertainment at short notice?"

Eddie thought for a moment. "Maybe thirty, I guess. There's only about fifty or sixty on the whole force."

"And how many would still volunteer if they knew it was a dangerous assignment?"

"At least as many. A lot of them are chafing at not getting to do 'real' police work."

"Great. Oh, and I'm going to need about the same number of men, but I assume that will be a lot easier. Tell the women they need to bring another cop as a date."

"I'll start making calls. But I don't know how you're going to get the department to let you use our resources for whatever you have in mind, even if it is to catch a murderer."

"I have an idea about that too."

We called Ginnie. We found her in her room, getting changed for lunch. I laid out the plan for her.

"I don't suppose your contacts extend to anybody senior in the LAPD?" I asked.

"Of course they do," she said. "I can give Clemence a call."

"Clemence Horrall?" I said, astonished. "The chief of police?" Although by now, I should have learned not to be astonished by the names Ginnie had in her little black book. "I can't imagine how much you had to donate to the widows and orphans to have that much clout."

"I have something much better," said Ginnie. "I know secrets about Clemence that would end his career."

"Gosh. Okay. Well, what about a location? It has to be tonight."

"I have just the thing. The Morocco club. We can rent it out for a private party. It has front and back doors, and several fire escape doors, I think. That should be enough for her, yes?"

"Won't that be expensive? I mean, even by your standards?"

"Not as much as you'd think. The club is usually completely dead in the middle of the week. I think they only keep it open that night because it's handy for money laundering."

"How does that work?" I asked. I didn't want to get too sidetracked, but I was curious, and it was going to bother me not to know.

"Let's say they only get a handful of guests on Wednesday night," Ginnie explained. "They write up the books as if they had a hundred and fifty people come through. Dirty money goes into the bank as what those made-up guests would have spent, and then comes out as payments for imaginary purchases of booze and food, wages for non-existent employees, inflated laundry bills, and so on. And just like that, dirty money becomes legitimate business profits."

The things I didn't know about the seedy underbelly of this city could fill a book. Or possibly a bookshop.

"We just have one more piece to complete the charade. If you can hang around for another hour, Joy and I will call you from the office."

"Okay, but I do have one condition," said Ginnie. "I want to be in the room when it all goes down this time."

"I really can't say no, can I?" I replied.

An hour later, Joy and I were at the office. We called up Ginnie to lay the bait.

"Ginnie," I said, "We've finally wrapped up the confidential case."

"Lovely. Is it time to celebrate?"

"Sort of. We have one in custody, but the other got away. So it's half a win."

"That's enough for a celebration for me. How about the Morocco club? Tonight at seven?"

"Perfect," I said, and we hung up.

"Let's hope McCardy gets that," I said.

Chapter Twenty

Joy, Ginnie, and I were ensconced in a corner of the Morocco with cocktails in front of us, eyes scanning the crowd for any sign of McCardy. Ginnie looked elegant as always, wearing a deep red dress with spaghetti straps, a low cut back, and a flared skirt. Joy looked good, and not too uncomfortable, in the clothes Ginnie had bought her for Palm Springs.

The club was small by LA nightclub standards, or 'intimate' as the owner would probably call it. The lighting was gently subdued, but not too dark. The sound system played Lena Horne's new album. Two dozen couples were sitting around circular tables or in booths. Waitresses wove among them, taking orders and delivering drinks. The level of chatter was comfortably low. It would have been a lovely evening if we weren't waiting for a killer to make an attempt on my life.

"I need to visit the powder room," I announced. Anxiety was doing weird things to my bladder.

"I'll get more drinks while you're gone," said Ginnie.

The ladies' room was decorated with expensive-looking wallpaper and large, Italian-looking floor tiles. It smelled faintly of a floral perfume, and the sound of the band could just about be heard through the door. It was one of the nicest bathrooms I had ever been in. There were five stalls. Only the one furthest from the door was occupied. I took the nearest one. When I was finished, I went over to the washbasin. I admired how neatly and consistently the towels were folded. It was the kind of thing that my brain liked to see. I had washed my hands and was touching up my lipstick when I heard the other stall door bang open. A face appeared in the mirror. I turned around.

"Hello Mary," I said. "I see you're a redhead now. It suits you."

"Thank you. I thought it was time to change up my look."

Her voice was as silky as before. I wondered whether she practiced that when she was alone. She was casually dangling her stiletto knife in her hand. I had no idea how I was going to talk my way out of this. Had I outsmarted myself?

"Have you been in here the whole time?" I said, trying to sound calm. "You're missing all the fun out there."

"Just thirty minutes, thank you for asking. I could have waited all night if necessary, though."

"What do you think of the nightclub?"

"It's a little clumsy for a trap, isn't? The cop pretending to be the bouncer is just about the only one who looks suited to his role. I noticed several more cops up and down the street outside, and a couple out back too. I assume there are people outside the fire exits."

"So what happens now?"

"I kill you, then I leave."

"How do you intend to do that without being stopped?"

"The same way I came in. I'll just walk through the club carrying a tray full of empty glasses, then through the kitchen and out the back. Nobody looks twice at waitresses," she said, smirking.

I took in her outfit. It wasn't exactly the same as the other waitresses were wearing, but it was close enough.

"I think you should know that every single customer out there is a police officer. The waitresses too. Even the barman is a retired cop who owns a bar. And all of them are looking for you. If you step through that door, yours will be the only face they don't recognize."

Her smile shifted slightly. Was that a cloud of doubt?

"I will just have to take my chances, I suppose," she said with a shrug. "Now if you prefer, I can kill you with a knife through the back of your neck. It's almost instant and supposedly quite painless. You just need to turn around and keep still."

"And if I refuse?"

"Then I'll have to do it the messy way. I'll stuff a towel in your mouth, then stab several of your vital organs and leave you to bleed out. It won't take too long, but it will be extremely painful the whole time."

"Is that the stiletto you killed Lewis with?"

"He was getting too noisy. And Wardour doesn't have the stomach for that sort of work any longer. Apparently, he can't even shoot somebody fifteen feet away."

"Would you do me one courtesy? At least tell me why the two of you did all this. Several people are dead, and I'd like to know why."

She smirked again. "For Mr. Wardour, it was simple. Sex and blackmail. In that order."

"I didn't see him as your type," I said. Even as the words were leaving my mouth, I questioned whether teasing her was such a good idea.

"Not me, you idiot," she replied. "Poor Mr. Wardour accidentally slept with a Soviet agent and told her things he shouldn't have, all about his bold adventures in Europe and what he was up to now. He was trying to impress her, I think. Anyway, the Soviets own him now."

"And you?"

"For me, it was simply about proving I could outsmart the rest of you."

I was thoroughly confused. "Why would you need to prove anything?"

"Because I used to be in SI too," she said. The silkiness was gone from her voice now. Sharp-edged anger had taken its place. "When OSS became CIG, they had to let a lot of people go. Of course, the women were at the top of the list. I managed to transfer into research and analysis, but only as a secretary. I risked my life for this country. And now I'm typing and filing for men who aren't even half as smart or as skilled as me. Burn-outs like Wardour and desk jockeys like Morgan. What did he ever risk? A paper cut?"

"I'm sure that's frustrating."

Lots of women feel the same way, I thought. *They don't sell out their country over it, though. Or murder people.*

"You have no idea. There were days when I fantasized about practicing my silent kill techniques on everybody in the office. So when I was offered a chance to show my worth to somebody who actually valued me, I leapt at it. Getting some payback on OSS at the same time was a bonus. And now I think it's time to conclude matters, before whatever cavalry you imagine is coming gets here."

At that moment the door creaked open, revealing Joy and, just behind her, Ginnie.

"We were wondering what—" began Joy, before recognizing McCardy.

McCardy swung around to point her knife towards the two of them. Instantly, I kicked her ankle as hard as I could, and she screamed. With her face contorted with rage, she started to turn back to me.

She was quick, but Joy was quicker. Her blackjack smacked into McCardy's wrist and she screamed even louder. McCardy's hand dangled at an impossible angle. The knife dropped to the floor and skittered across the tiles. She dove for it, but was too slow again. Ginnie's stiletto heel was pinning the blade to the floor. For a moment, she scrabbled uselessly at it with her left hand, then rolled over onto her back and cradled her broken right wrist, moaning quietly.

I pulled handcuffs from my purse. "This is probably going to hurt a great deal," I said, "and I'm not sorry at all."

The next morning, we gathered at the police station. McCardy, her broken wrist in a cast, was in a holding cell alongside Wardour. Sam, moving carefully to avoid tearing his stitches, and Frankie had joined us.

"What do you intend to do with them now?" Daniel asked Eddie.

"For a start," said Eddie, "you all need to provide statements. You and Frankie need to explain about being kidnapped, and Sam, obviously, about being stabbed. That should be plenty to hold them on while we figure out the rest. But I don't know what to do about the spying charges."

"Shouldn't you hand them over to the FBI?" asked Joy. "I thought espionage was their jurisdiction."

"And let them take all the credit for our work? No way!"

"Um, look," said Daniel, "could we perhaps not do either of those things?"

"Why not?" said Eddie.

"Because if there's an arrest and a trial, it will be extremely damaging to the credibility of the bureau, whether it's the LAPD or the FBI taking the credit. The bureau barely survived OSS being disbanded. I don't know if it can survive this."

"What then?"

"Help me deliver them to the CIG. Let them handle it internally. We have, well, stronger interrogation techniques, let's say, than are available to you. They're both trained to resist questioning, and I doubt that anything you can do legally will get anything out of them. Give them to CIG, and I assure you, they will get what they deserve."

"How do you figure that?"

"OSS was military, remember. They can be recalled to the army, then quietly court-martialled. We can bring in evidence about their spying in a closed trial that we could never expose in open court. And then they will disappear into Leavenworth for a very long time.

Eddie was silent for a full minute. "Very well," he said. "But you're going to owe me a huge favor for this."

"You mean on top of what I owe you all for saving my life?" replied Daniel.

Chapter Twenty-one

One week later, Joy, Daniel, and I found ourselves sat around a table at Café del Sol.

"How have you been?" asked Joy.

"I've been debriefing with different people all week," said Daniel. "And I spent this morning with the CIG regional director. I gave him an overview of the whole business. He's very impressed by how we all handled it, even though we broke a few rules along the way. Mind you, breaking rules and improvising in field ops is very on-brand for OSS. And he's very grateful to you all for keeping it out of the press and especially away from the FBI. As for me personally, I don't know how I can ever repay you."

"One detail has been bugging me. Did you ever figure out how they got their bogus production set up?"

"It turns out it wasn't too complicated. They faked some paperwork—production sheets, booking sheets, executive approval memos, and so on—then broke in one night and inserted it all into the right inbox in the production department. The next day, lots of people were helpfully setting up soundstage fourteen for principal photography on *Berlin Skies*, including a nice big sign on the outside, no questions asked."

"And nobody wondered about it?"

"In a company that size, it's easy for everybody to assume it's somebody else's project. When you think about it, it's a great place to hide in plain sight, come and go as you please, and keep the doors locked to everybody else. It seems they'd been looking at framing me as their exit strategy for some time."

"Wow. Anyway, where's the investigation at now?" I asked.

"McCardy and Wardour are being interrogated by X-2," he replied.

I suppose he saw our blank looks.

"The counter-intelligence branch of CIG," he explained. "But not surprisingly, so far, they're not telling us much we don't already know. They won't give up their Soviet handler. Give it time."

"Any progress on figuring out who killed Barbara? Or Ted Lewis?"

"They both blame Lewis for the hit-and-run on Barbara, and honestly, it seems plausible. Just to be thorough, we checked the dates of Hathaway's two dented fenders, and they don't match."

"I guess he really is just a lousy driver," I replied. "And the killing of Lewis?"

"They are each blaming the other, despite what McCardy confessed to you. Neither has an alibi for the night he was killed, so we might never know who did it. They probably think they can both get off this way, but we'll just charge both of them for it as a conspiracy."

"Why did they kill him, though?" asked Joy. "Wasn't he working for them?"

"They say that he was becoming too uncontrollable. He killed Barbara without clearing it with them first. The attack on Caroline—which, by the way, was supposed to be you, Dot—was also the result of him acting without instructions. When he came out here to LA in pursuit of you, they decided he was too much of a risk to keep around any longer."

"And what about Rolf?"

"Well, here's an odd thing. They both deny knowing anything about that. They said they didn't even know who he was. And I think I believe them."

"Why?" asked Joy.

"They're already on the hook for killing Lewis, for my attempted murder, for kidnapping Frankie, and for enough treasonous acts to put them away for life. So why not come clean on that one?"

"Another one of Lewis's freelance jobs, maybe?" said Joy.

"I have a different theory," I said. "And it's a loose end we really need to tie up."

"What's that?" asked Daniel.

"In all this chaos, we never got a chance to talk about Schäfer."

"You're right. Do you think he's part of the ring too?"

"I don't see how he would fit in with McCardy and Wardour's operation. If they had him, they wouldn't have needed Lewis. His access is much better, and he isn't so much of a loose cannon. Tell me, is it at all possible that there were two separate Soviet operations on the base?"

"Very possible. The military intelligence and state intelligence organizations hate each other, perhaps even more than they hate us. They even have agents infiltrating each other's organizations. GRU—that's the military side—thinks it has a monopoly on foreign operations. The civilians don't agree. So yes, especially for something as big as Paperclip, it's highly plausible that they were running parallel, competing operations. So talk to me about Schäfer."

"There's two things about him that I don't like. The first is that suitcase with the tamper-evident lock."

"Was the lock really shoddy?" asked Daniel. "Like it might fall apart if you looked at it the wrong way?"

"Yes. How did you know?"

"That's a bad sign. The Soviets use them all the time; they mass produce them. They're very poor quality, but they're a deterrent in some circumstances, I suppose. You said two things, what's the other one?"

"He speaks English with an excellent accent. Not American, though. British. Every other German on the base, in fact, almost every other German I've ever heard, speaks with an obvious German accent."

Daniel furrowed his brow. "Oh, that's very bad. Soviet agents study English listening to BBC short wave radio, so they typically all acquire BBC accents. It's circumstantial, but it's very concerning. But how would the Soviets get a scientist into Paperclip?"

"I have a theory about that too, concerning those German scientists that you scooped up in the Soviet zone. Is it possible the Soviets planted agents among them? For instance, Germans who had been working for them during the war, spying on German military research?"

Daniel groaned. "That's exactly what they would do if they realized we were poaching on their territory. Now we have to go back and take another look at everybody we brought from the Soviet zone. So you're saying Schäfer killed Rolf?"

"I think so. But I don't think he acted alone. He and Lewis were both concerned about my investigation. It would make sense that they briefly set aside their differences for their mutual benefit. Maybe Lewis told Schäfer about my progress, and that if he could provide a suitable scapegoat among the Germans, it would give his handlers an excuse to shut me down. And since Schäfer hated Rolf, he was the obvious choice."

"Do you think anybody else was working with Schäfer?"

"Well, that's tricky," I said. "Can I ask you something off the record?"

"Not if it's material to the case," he replied. "Not even for you. Sorry."

"Perhaps you could ask a hypothetical question," suggested Joy.

"But it's not a hypothetic- Oh. Right."

Daniel smiled. "A hypothetical question would be just fine, and would not need to be part of the record."

"Suppose somebody was being coerced into working for Schäfer. Perhaps they came here from a country now under Soviet occupation, and their parents are still back there and are being threatened. What might happen to that person?"

"If X-2 got hold of them, they'd probably want to play them back."

"I don't know what that means."

"It means they would leave them in place, and use them to send low-grade intelligence to maintain the deception but mix in fake reports to mislead their research. Schäfer would be threatened into helping. And whatever requests the Soviets might send to Schäfer would be useful intel for us. It tells us what they're working on and where they are weak."

"How long would that go on?"

"For as long as they could get away with it. Years, perhaps."

"If the Soviets were to figure out that the person was being played back, it sounds like it would be very bad for the parents. Hypothetically."

"Yes, it would."

"What if X-2 didn't know, but you did? Could you do something to help them? Maybe get the parents out?"

"You're thinking of a prisoner swap? Schäfer for the parents? Things like that do get done from time to time. It would depend on how badly they want Schäfer back. With the operation blown, the parents have no value to the Soviets. And if Schäfer has intel they don't want us to get out of him, they would probably be willing to trade for him."

"Would you do that for me? Ali is a good friend and she's in a spot."

"I'll take it to my Regional Director. After everything you've done for us, it's certainly worth asking. And frankly, it would be nice to end my time here on a positive achievement."

"What does that mean, end your time here?" I asked.

"When this case is wrapped up, I'm leaving the bureau."

"I'm astonished," I said. "When we first met, you seemed so committed to your work."

He sighed heavily. "I was. But something you said when we first met touched me. You said that the war was over and you had a life now. I deserve to have a life too. One where I can tell my friends what I do for living and my colleagues aren't ghosts when we leave the office. Then this whole business—discovering that my two closest colleagues were Soviet spies and I didn't even notice—made me question everything. If I stay at the bureau, I'll be forever looking over my shoulder and wondering who else is a traitor. And it feels like there's a new war coming, not a war of soldiers and guns, but a cold war of spies and lies. I want no part of it. Not if it means making moral choices like Project Paperclip."

"We won the war, but maybe we're losing ourselves in the peace," said Joy. It was a depressing prospect.

"What are you going to do instead?" I said to Daniel. "I can't imagine a lot of other uses for your skillset."

"There's a new thing that's started up, called Project RAND," replied Daniel, smiling now. "It's a blend of the kind of operational research we created during the war with systems analysis and a bunch of other analytical skills. Lots of very smart people are involved. It's a fantastic place and a friend of mine from the old days has tapped me to come on board." The excitement was evident in his voice.

"It sounds like a fresh start is just what you need," said Joy. "So where will you be based?"

"Santa Monica," he said, grinning. "Just up the road. So we can meet for coffee any time we want."

"That sounds perfect," I replied. "But there's one more thing."

Daniel waited expectantly.

"Now that this is all over, at least as far as we are concerned, will we ever be able to tell anybody about it?"

"Well, technically, the case was over when Wardour shut it down, and that was the end of your obligation to confidentiality. Everything that's happened after that is your own story to tell as you see fit. But obviously, I would prefer if the story didn't spread too widely. I still care what happens to my colleagues in the bureau."

"Is telling Ginnie okay?"

"Yes. Ginnie is okay."

Daniel decided that his work could stand to wait another half hour, and ordered another round of coffee. I stared into mine but didn't drink it. I thought about everything Daniel had said. I felt sour about Project Paperclip too. What was the good in winning if it meant betraying the very principles we were fighting for?

I felt even worse about the case. Whatever Daniel told me, I felt like Barbara was dead because I hadn't taken the case. And Rolf was dead because I had. I did not feel like the hero of my own story.

Epilogue

Spring turned to summer. Life resumed its regular cadence. We dealt with cases that didn't have Nazis, Soviets, spies, traitors, or classified military secrets. My undercover assignment with Daniel became just another file in our filing cabinet, albeit a highly redacted one. The press had gotten a sniff of two intelligence agents being arrested for treason, but knew nothing of the details. Our names didn't come up. With little to feed the story, public interest faded and turned instead to red-baiting rumors of Communists infiltrating Hollywood. It wasn't clear to me what their goal would be if they succeeded. Perhaps they would agitate for a sympathetic biopic about Stalin.

And then one warm, perfect Los Angeles summer morning in June, the bell of the outer door rang. I opened the office door to find a familiar face standing in our waiting room. Ali.

"Very nice bookshop you have, Dot," she said.

She looked tired, worn, and more lined around the face, but nonetheless, there was a small smile around her lips. I went over and gave her a brief hug, then called for Joy to come out of the office. I introduced them. Joy gave Ali a much longer hug.

"Did you fly or take the Greyhound?" Joy asked.

"The bus. It took four days," replied Ali.

"No wonder you look tired. Let's go get a drink and you can tell us all about it."

"But it is so early to drink. There is a bar open at this time?" said Ali.

Joy laughed lightly. "We know a bar that's always open."

"And besides," I added, "it's lunchtime in Ohio."

We walked over to Jack's and settled ourselves around a high-top.

"How did you find me?" I asked Ali.

"An old copy of Yellow Pages. Your bookshop is listed in it, so I think, let me see what is there now. Perhaps a neighbor knows where you go. And yet here you are, a private detective."

"More to the point, why are you here?"

I had no idea how much Ali knew, in particular about my role, what Daniel had told her, or what she had figured out for herself.

"I came to thank you in person for helping me. Also to return your shoes."

"Morgan told you about me?"

"He told me almost nothing. Compartmentalization, he said. Difficult word! But I'm sure you made it happen. You were undercover, yes, investigating Schäfer?"

"Yes, I was." She didn't need to know the rest.

"And when you lied about your mother being sick, you were letting me know, yes? To tell to me you knew I was in trouble and would still try to help, but so nobody else would know."

"Yes. I picked up your own lie about what Schäfer was angry about. Joy suggested that it might be a coded request for help without any risk of Schäfer finding out. So I tried to respond in kind."

"Is it really okay that I am here now?"

"Of course. I genuinely meant it when I said to come and visit me. I don't make a lot of friends, so the ones I do make I value dearly, and try to hold on to."

I looked across at Joy. She slipped off her chair, came around the table, and gave me a brief hug. I didn't mind too much. When she took her seat again, I might have had a tiny little tear in the corner of my eye.

"Anyway," I continued, "is there any news of your parents?"

"Mr. Morgan said the trade is agreed, my parents for Schäfer, but it can still take a long time to happen. He says that with the Soviets, nothing happens for weeks and then they call and say, 'We do it tomorrow, in Vienna!'"

"What will you do now?" Joy asked.

"I don't know. I cannot work in intelligence again. They say I am compromised. It makes no sense."

"Trust me, nothing in intelligence makes much sense," I replied.

"So I have another job now, in an office. I have secretary skills, how hard can it be? In a few days, I go back to Dayton."

"Why not stay? The weather's a lot nicer here," said Joy. "We can help you get set up."

"Actually, I have an idea about that," I said. "No promises, though."

Three hours later, we joined Ginnie in the lounge at the Marmont, a half-drunk cocktail in front of her. Ali was wearing her sleek dress from the Valentine's party, and the shoes I had lent her. I had told her to keep them. I knew I would soon be getting more.

I made the introductions.

"Ginnie, this is Ali Barbinski. Ali, this is Ginnie, the sponsor behind our agency, a regular provider of business leads, and most of all, a very good friend," I said.

We ordered a round of drinks. Ginnie persuaded Ali to try a vodka martini instead of her habitual straight vodka.

"Ali?" said Ginnie. "Short for Alicja?"

Ali smiled broadly. "You are first American who pronounces it correctly!" she said.

"Well, you're not the first Alicja I've met. During the war, I started a refugee resettlement charity here, and we're still going strong. A lot of people are trying to get out of the Soviet occupied territories, and most of them arrive with nothing but the clothes they're wearing and often, little or no English."

"Well, you're full of surprises," exclaimed Joy. "I did not know that."

"Anyway," said Ginnie, "there's a whole Polish diaspora here. If you're staying a while, I can introduce you."

"Oh, that would be wonderful. It would be nice to hear Polish again. And perhaps I can help teach English?"

"If you're going to be around long enough, that would be lovely."

"That sort of brings us to why we're here on such short notice," I said. "Ali is looking for work. And we need an office manager. She can free us up from a lot of secretarial and admin tasks, which means we can spend more time on billable work. And with somebody in the office full time, we won't miss out on potential jobs because a customer called or visited when we were both out."

"That sounds like an excellent idea all round," said Ginnie. "The additional business you'll be able to do will certainly offset the cost. And it will look so much more professional."

Ali looked delighted.

"Is it okay to hug?" she said.

Ginnie nodded. Ali went around the table and gave her a hug so long and so tight it made me uncomfortable just to watch.

"Well," said Ginnie, "I think this calls for another round of drinks!"

Author's Note

To the best of my ability, historical details are as accurate as I could make them while still serving the story. There really was a Project Paperclip, and research into jet aircraft by German scientists and engineers was based at Wright Field. And the intelligence services did cover up the war crimes of scientists considered sufficiently valuable to the project.

The techniques, organization, and history of the OSS mentioned here are also largely historically correct. The Central Intelligence Group became the CIA shortly after the events of this story. The Bureau of Intelligence and Research, known as INR, still exists, and is highly regarded among the intelligence community.

Clemence Horrall was LAPD chief of police from 1941 until 1949, when he was forced to resign due to a corruption scandal that led him to perjure himself before a grand jury. It emerged that he had long been aware that several of his officers had been protecting a madam named Brenda Allen, who ran a prostitution syndicate that counted many of LA's wealthiest and most powerful residents among its clients. The scandal provided the thrust for a major cleanup of the LAPD under his replacement as chief.

And finally, Hedy Lamarr really was extremely intelligent.

ABOUT THE AUTHOR

J.T. Berry has carefully avoided the kinds of jobs and adventures that make authors sound interesting in these biographies, apart perhaps from that one time in Czechoslovakia. After a first career that involved lots of office cubicles and slide presentations, J.T. is now attempting to make a living as a writer. This is the third book in the D'Amico and Stone mystery series.